Jennifer D. Bokal is the author of the bestselling ancient-world historical romance *The Gladiator's Mistress* and the second book in the Champions of Rome series, *The Gladiator's Temptation*. Happily married to her own alpha male for twenty years, she enjoys writing stories that explore the wonders of love in many genres. Jen and her husband live in upstate New York with their three beautiful daughters, two aloof cats and two very spoiled dogs.

Also by Jennifer D. Bokal

Her Rocky Mountain Defender
Her Rocky Mountain Hero

Discover more at millsandboon.co.uk

HER ROCKY MOUNTAIN DEFENDER

JENNIFER D. BOKAL

MILLS & BOON

First Published in Great Britain 2018
by Mills & Boon, an imprint of HarperCollins*Publishers*
1 London Bridge Street, London, SE1 9GF

Her Rocky Mountain Defender © 2018 Jennifer D. Bokal

ISBN: 978-0-263-26570-5

39-0418

MIX
Paper from
responsible sources
FSC™ C007454

This book is produced from independently certified FSC™ paper to ensure responsible forest management.

For more information visit: www.harpercollins.co.uk/green

Printed and bound in Spain
by CPI, Barcelona

As always, this book is dedicated to John.
Twenty years of marriage has taught me to hope,
to laugh and, most important—to love.

Prologue

Roman DeMarco sat at the table in the kitchen of a cramped studio apartment. Like an ever-present fog, the smell of overcooked eggs crept in from the hallway. In the distance, a baby's wail pierced the still afternoon. He lifted his weary gaze to the window. The view was of the stained brick building next door. Roman had lived under an alias—Roman Black—paying rent and sleeping in this apartment for almost half of a year, yet this place wasn't his home.

Turning his gaze back to the table, Roman held up his latest creation. It was a powerful ELD, or electronic listening device. He hit the power button. A small rectangular screen glowed and filled with boxy script. It held two words: Signal Obtained.

During his years as an intelligence officer with Delta Force, Roman had bugged many rooms. But this next target had proved to be uniquely difficult.

As far as Roman was concerned, he loved the challenge. The targeted room—underground and made of concrete—was the first problem. Any signal coming from the room needed to be strong, and using an easily hidden, thumb-size ELD was impossible. It left Roman to fashion his own device. The bug might be larger than he wanted, but the battery should be powerful enough to last fourteen days. Or so he hoped.

"Testing. Testing. One. Two. Three," he said.

He pressed a small button on the side. His words were replayed. "Testing. Testing. One. Two. Three."

He turned the device over and examined the back. Two powerful magnets lined each side of the ELD. He moved to his refrigerator and held out the black box. Like a live thing, the magnets pulled, and the ELD wiggled in his grasp. He let go and it sailed an inch from his hand, connecting with the appliance's metal casing. He smiled to himself. If things went as planned, Roman was about to reclaim his former life.

It couldn't come a day too soon.

Chapter 1

Boulder, Colorado.
9:45 PM
May 5

"There you go," Roman DeMarco said. He poured whiskey into a shot glass and slid the drink to a customer. Moving to the next person, he cast his gaze at the room. It was still early in the evening, but more than two dozen patrons filled The Prow.

No, *patron* wasn't the right word; it gave the bar an air of respectability it didn't deserve. This place was the last stop on a person's long, downhill slide to the gutter. Only a few recessed lights over the bar illuminated the windowless room. The smell of stale beer, body odor and desperation hung in the air. The constant *thump, thump, thump* of a rock song pounded through the stereo system, the bass so deep that the sticky floor reverberated with the chords. The occasional cackle of drunken laughter cut through the music—the sound more manic than merry.

Singles hunched protectively over their drinks, while couples cast furtive glances at each other and moved toward darkened corners. The words, *The Prow*—spelled out in neon letters three feet high— were superimposed on the front of an illuminated sailing ship as it cut through a glowing wave. The sign hung on the back wall and cast a bloody light on a motorcycle club shooting a game of pool.

It would have been easy for Roman to feel disdain for these people, the forgotten of the world. But he didn't, not at all.

He wasn't your average bartender. No, as an employee of Rocky Mountain Justice, a private security firm, Roman was at The Prow to gather information about the bar's owner, Oleg Zavalov.

Five months prior, RMJ had gained information about Nikolai Mateev, a Russian drug lord who was wanted all over the world. The recent intel suggested that Zavalov not only laundered money for Mateev, but employed his great-nephew, as well. But what RMJ needed was proof—and that meant putting one of their people on the inside. With dual specialties in electronic surveillance and languages, Roman was the perfect man for the job.

It was hard to break through, though. Zavalov, mistrustful by nature, kept a tightly knit duo of two Russian nationals with him all the time. One of them was indeed Nikolai Mateev's great-nephew. Beyond that, in five months Roman had gleaned woefully little information about the suspected money laundering. Yet, he hoped that once he planted that ELD in Oleg Zavalov's office, all of that would change.

Now all he needed was an excuse to get into the locked basement and plant the bug.

A regular, a cop who drank for free, approached and slammed down an empty glass. "Another beer," he said, running a hand through his thick blond hair. Worse than anyone else was the cop who turned a blind eye to the rampant crime in this place for free beer.

Roman faked a smile.

"Sure," he said, grabbing the glass. He turned to the tap and pulled down the handle. Foam spit and gurgled from the tap. An empty keg was the perfect reason to get into the basement.

"This one's spent, Jackson," he said to the cop. Jackson. Roman could never figure out if it was a first or last name. "Give me a minute. I need to get a new keg from the basement," Roman said, turning to the manager as Jackson shifted his attention to a group of women nearby.

The manager held out a ring with three keys and Roman took them with a nod. He unlocked the basement door marked as private, and flipped on the light switch. The golden glow of a single bulb illuminated a set of dilapidated wooden stairs, cinder block walls and a patch of gunmetal-gray concrete of the basement floor.

A hallway with four doors was laid out at the bottom of the stairs. The back door, controlled with an electronic lock, led to the alley behind the bar. On the left there was a locked door to the beer cooler and next door, a storage room filled with cheap liquor and stale snacks. The final door, the one that led to Oleg Zavalov's office, was on the right.

Roman didn't waste any time. He quickly unlocked Zavalov's office door and slipped inside. Using the penlight he kept in his back pocket, he withdrew the ELD and powered up the device. A small green screen began to glow. One word appeared: Acquiring.

"Damn." He moved closer to the door. Still no connection. He glanced at his watch. He'd been gone less than two minutes, but how much longer before his absence was noticed upstairs?

The inset screen still glowed green as one word scrolled across its face.

Acquiring.

Acquiring.

The sound of footsteps on the stairs drew his attention. He glanced at the screen one last time. Signal Obtained. Roman placed the ELD under the top of

Zavalov's desk, an imperfect place, but the best option he had. The door creaked open, giving Roman a split second to think up an excuse for being in a room that was unquestionably off-limits.

Madelyn Thompkins wasn't in the habit of sneaking down rickety staircases in dive bars. But this was the opposite of habit: according to social media, her sister, Ava had been at The Prow less than an hour before.

No one had heard from Ava since she checked out of rehab in their hometown of Cheyenne, Wyoming, four months ago. So to have her turn up in Boulder, where Madelyn was enrolled in med school? It was an opportunity she couldn't squander.

Despite the crummy neighborhood and the sketchy bar, Madelyn came straightaway. A quick search of both the main bar and the bathroom turned up nothing. It left her with two choices: give up on her first chance in months to find her sister, or explore the entire building—even the parts that were off-limits, like the basement hallway she was standing in. Then again, when she thought of it that way, Madelyn didn't have a choice at all.

She pushed the slightly ajar door fully open and peered into the room. A figure, shrouded with the dark, moved. *She wasn't alone.* Her pulse spiked and she bit her bottom lip to keep it from quivering.

"Hello," she called out. The room swallowed her

words. "I'm looking for Ava Thompkins. Do you know her?"

"You aren't supposed to be here. This place is for employees only," a man said. "The sign on the door says 'Private.' Can't you read?"

She hadn't come this way for nothing. She fished her phone from her cross-body purse and pulled up her sister's latest picture and post. Turning the screen to the room, she asked, "Do you recognize this woman?"

Suddenly the man was in front of her. He had short, dark hair, and was clad in a form-fitting black T-shirt and snug jeans. He was big—well over six feet tall with broad shoulders and muscular arms. The outline of his pecs and abs were unmistakable.

"I'm the bartender, so I see a lot of people," he said, giving a noncommittal answer. "What's she to you?"

"My sister." Holding the phone at arm's length, Madelyn continued, "She was here less than an hour ago. You must've seen her."

"Why do you care?"

"Besides her being my sister? Isn't that enough?"

"Not always."

Madelyn hesitated only a little before sharing Ava's history. "She checked out of rehab and we haven't heard from her since."

"Maybe she doesn't want to be found," the bartender said.

"I doubt she does," said Madelyn. "But I'm desperate to find her."

"Like I said, lots of folks come and go." He gave a useless shrug. "I don't remember them all."

"Are you sure?" Even to her own ears, Madelyn's voice was tight and thin, like a string about to break. She wasn't going to let Ava slip away again, not when this man might be able to help. "You've never seen her before?"

"You seem like a nice lady, so I'm going to be honest with you. This isn't a nice bar. Just go home. It's safer for you there."

"If it's not safe for me, then it's not safe for my sister."

"Go." The man pointed toward the stairs.

"Why are you trying to get rid of me?"

"Why are you being so difficult to get rid of?" The man grabbed her elbow. "Let me walk you to your car," he said. "If your sister stops in, I'll let her know that you're looking for her."

Madelyn's joy soared, taking her to a dizzying height. While he might not be the key to finding her sister, the bartender was a link in the chain that led to Ava.

"You know her?" Madelyn asked.

"She's been around."

Standing on the threshold, it occurred to Madelyn that the man hadn't bothered to turn on the light in the darkened room behind him. Was he trying to hide something? She eased around him, entering the room. "Where is she?"

The man stepped in Madelyn's way, blocking her

from gaining further access. "I don't know where your sister is now," he said. "But I do know that she's not in this office."

Madelyn narrowed her eyes.

He held up two fingers and said, "Scout's honor."

"You? A Boy Scout? I thought you said that nobody nice came to The Prow."

"Would you believe me if I told you that I made Eagle Scout by the time I turned sixteen years old?"

For an inexplicable reason, Madelyn did. "So, Boy Scout, why won't you help a hardworking doctor find her ill sister?"

"You're a doctor?"

She corrected herself, "Well, I'm not a doctor—not yet, anyway. But I am a medical school student at the University of Colorado." A flush crept from her chest to her cheeks as Madelyn realized she'd rambled.

Maybe it would be for the best if she just went home.

The bartender closed the space between them. His spicy scent surrounded her and she drew in a deep breath.

Her eyes had adjusted to the light and for the first time she looked at his large frame closely. His short hair had lighter streaks throughout and Madelyn wondered if he spent time in the sun. Dark stubble covered his cheeks, and still she could see the cleft in his chin. The collar of his black T-shirt was frayed.

"So, what kind of doctor are you?" he asked.

Madelyn didn't want the flirtation to continue, yet she found herself saying, "I'm thinking of specializing in psychiatry."

"Because of your sister?" he asked. "And her addiction."

"Who sounds like a shrink now?" Madelyn joked.

"Listen."

Madelyn tried to think of something charming, or at least witty, to retort. But she stopped. The bartender held himself as if he were forged from iron and not flesh and blood. He had not been teasing, he truly wanted her to *listen*. Then she heard them— male voices speaking, but not English. Ukrainian? Or Russian, maybe?

The man placed his mouth next to her ear, his breath hot on her skin. "Those men are going to walk through that door in one minute and neither one of us should be in this office. I want to protect you, but to do that I need to give them a reason why we're trespassing."

"Protect me?" His words were more confusing than menacing. "What do you mean?"

"I'm on your side," he assured her, "but what's your name?"

"Madelyn," she said. "My name is Madelyn Thompkins."

"Madelyn," the man said, pulling her closer still, "I'm Roman."

"Why do I need to know who you are?"

"Because as an Eagle Scout, I'm honor bound to introduce myself to any distressed damsels that I kiss."

Roman wrapped his arms around Madelyn's waist and pulled her to him. She gave a little mew of surprise. The kiss was for show and at the same time, blood pounded at the base of Roman's skull with his desire for more. He didn't mind all the hours spent alone, but damn—holding Madelyn felt good, like he truly had come home.

Even though it hadn't been part of his plan, Roman slid his tongue into her mouth. She pushed at him, her hands splayed against his chest. Yet as the kiss deepened and she returned the ardor, the tension in her arms relaxed and her body formed to his.

Overhead, the light blazed to life.

"Roman Black." The alias always sounded foreign to his ears, yet he recognized the person who spoke as The Prow's owner, Oleg Zavalov. "What the hell's going on here?"

Roman broke away from the kiss. He did so reluctantly—as if forced to stop something he enjoyed—and it wasn't exactly an act.

Oleg Zavalov stood in the doorway. Hair slicked back, he wore a tailored suit, along with a button-down shirt, open at the throat. He was flanked by his two underlings from Russia, Anton and Serge. Both men were tall and broad and stupid, a complete contrast to Oleg. And Roman was certain that one of them was Nikolai's great-nephew.

"Oleg." Roman pulled Madelyn into his chest. "Sorry about using your office. We just needed a moment of privacy and the beer cooler didn't seem like a classy place to take a lady."

Oleg always had a beautiful woman or two hanging off his arm. So Roman knew that he'd never begrudge anyone a quick hookup.

With a shake of his head, Oleg clapped Roman on the shoulder. "I knew you'd eventually find someone you liked. Next time use the stockroom like everyone else."

"Sure," said Roman. His eye went to the place where he'd hastily planted the ELD. He forced himself to look away. Grabbing Madelyn's hand, he led her to the door and into the hallway.

"Hey, Black," Oleg called.

He turned. Oleg sat on the edge of his desk. His leg swung lazily back and forth and his rear was settled right above the ELD.

Roman began to sweat. "Yeah?"

"They need a keg upstairs. Get the beer to the bar and then if you want a break, take one."

Silently, Anton and Serge slipped into the office. Like twin pillars of brute force, they took up positions at opposite sides of the door.

"Sure," Roman said. "I'll take care of the beer right away."

Roman's hand remained on Madelyn's back. Her muscles tensed under his touch. He assumed she was sensitive to the implication of what a *break* entailed and he hated that she might see him as creep.

For the first time in months, Roman wanted to explain himself to someone—to Madelyn, specifically. To hell with his undercover work, he needed her to see him as the good guy and not a part of all this, the criminal underbelly of Boulder.

His hand still on Madelyn's back, he led her to the stairs. That ELD wasn't going to stay hidden for long and the best Roman could hope for was another chance to reposition it later in the night.

But first, he needed to get Madelyn out of the bar and make sure she was safe. She ascended the stairs. One. Two. Three. He followed close behind. As her foot landed on the fourth step, a metallic *thunk* filed from the office and swept into the corridor.

The ELD really hadn't stayed hidden for long.

"Run," he whispered into Madelyn's ear.

She took the remaining steps two at a time, Roman on her heels.

"What the hell?" There was a moment of silence and then Oleg began to curse. "Roman!" he bellowed.

Roman didn't bother to slow his stride or answer.

"Get back here."

Roman felt an invisible target between his shoulder blades. He imagined one on Madelyn's, as well.

"Roman!"

Roman had very few options. Run, and get shot in the back. Or stay, and be murdered in Oleg's office. Neither appealed, but he refused to be taken down without a fight.

With the door just two steps away, Roman reached around Madelyn to grip the handle. A familiar click resounded through the hallway. Such a small noise, insignificant and yet so momentous that it reverberated in his chest. It was the unmistakable sound of a gun's safety being released.

Madelyn's thoughts were disjointed and jumbled all at once. She could barely comprehend what had just happened. The men. Their guns. Icy terror clawing at her throat. A strong arm pushing open the door. Rushing into the bar, she stumbled on the last step. The same strong arm lifted her and ushered her forward. She ran, stumbling again as she heard a crack, the whiff of sulfur, followed by buzzing in her ears.

She looked over her shoulder, and the continuum of time began to flow again. The men with the guns were right behind her. One stood, his weapon drawn, a tendril of smoke swirling from the barrel. Roman, the man who'd kissed her—warned her about this bar—turned back. He lifted a bar stool and brought it around. It crashed into the man with a gun. He teetered. The firearm flew from his grasp. The second man lifted his arm, gun in hand. Roman delivered a kick to his knee and the shooter crumpled to the floor. Frightened bar patrons scattered to the corners of the room.

"Roman," she screamed.

The first man had risen to his knees and was reaching for his gun. Roman planted one foot on the outstretched hand. His other foot connected with the man's chin. Blood sprayed from his mouth as his head snapped back. The second man was unsteady, but up. He leveled his gun with Roman's chest. Without thought, Madelyn lifted a glass from the bar and threw. It hit the man in the shoulder. There wasn't adequate force to knock him down, just enough to ruin his aim.

"Get the hell out of here," Roman said to her.

Madelyn didn't need to be told twice. Pivoting, she sprinted to the door. She pushed it open and took in one gulping breath of clean, fresh air. But then...

An arm encircled her waist. Her lungs emptied in a gasp and her feet dangled above the floor.

"Hold on there. You aren't going anywhere." The stench of beer breath and cologne washed over her. Acidic fear rose in the back of her throat.

Madelyn grabbed the hand that held her, wrenching back the fingers. They didn't budge. She bucked and kicked, swinging out legs and arms. Sweat trickled down her back. The grip around her middle tightened.

"Let me go," she said. "You can't do this. I'll call the police."

"Police?" The man who held her snorted. "I am the police."

The door was still so close. If she reached out,

she could graze the handle. But even if she did, it would do her no good. Like a pinprick in a balloon, the fight leaked out of Madelyn.

"Let her go," said another man. Madelyn recognized Oleg, the guy who found them in the basement.

The arm around her middle released and Madelyn fell to the floor. She looked over her shoulder. Roman, bloodied and bruised, knelt a few feet away. One of the thugs held his shoulder. The other pointed a gun at Roman's head. The rest of the people in the bar only stared, not bothering to offer aid or even turn their impassive gazes away.

"Just a little misunderstanding," said Oleg with a wave and smile. "We're going to go downstairs and clear it all up. Until then, the next round is on the house."

This pronouncement was greeted with a weak cheer.

The man who had caught her, grabbed her arm and dragged her toward the basement door. Madelyn searched every face in the bar for one person who would help—do something, anything. Speak up or call the police. Then she remembered, the person who now held her was a cop. Dear God, this could not be happening. All she wanted to do was find her sister.

Oleg stopped at the door and placed his hand on the middle of the cop's chest. "Thanks for your help, Jackson," he said. "I've got it from here."

"Sure," said Jackson, "no problem. I'm on duty soon, anyway."

Jackson. Madelyn would never forget his name. She studied his face and memorized every detail— his height, six feet three inches, or maybe six foot four, athletic build, the exact shade of his blond hair. How his right eye was slightly bigger than his left, and one tooth on the bottom leaned a little on its neighbor. The more information she had, the better a description she could give later.

Oleg grabbed her arm, his fingers dug into her flesh. He pulled Madelyn across the threshold and the door closed with a crack. A thought snapped into place and her mouth went dry. None of these men had hidden their appearance. They weren't worried about what she might say, because as far as they were concerned—she wasn't leaving The Prow alive.

Madelyn yanked her arm free. Escape. Escape. Escape. Her fingertips brushed the cold, metal handle. Oleg grabbed her arm again, pulling her away. She pitched back. Her skull slammed into the stairs, turning everything dark and then filling her head with light and pain. Her feet flew up, sending her somersaulting downward. Her shoulder hit the concrete floor and her vision flashed with red. Her body ached with each beat of her heart.

"Madelyn." Roman placed a strong hand under her elbow, helping her to sit up. "Madelyn, are you okay?"

She was as far away from okay as she could get. "What's happening? Why is this happening?"

Roman lightly rubbed his hand over her shoulder. "She's got nothing to do with us, Oleg. Let her go."

"Nothing? She shows up and I find this." Oleg reached into the interior pocket of his jacket and withdrew a small, plastic box. He knelt in front of Madelyn. "Who do you work for? How'd you get him to betray me?"

"I've never seen that thing before in my life. I don't even know what that is. Roman?"

"She's nobody, just a girl," said Roman. "It's me, all along, it's been me."

"Search them both."

One of the thugs pawed through Madelyn's purse and patted her roughly from shoulders to feet. From Roman, they got a set of keys from his pocket.

Oleg held the keys in his palm. "So, you use my own business to betray me? After I brought you in and gave you a job." He threw the keys to one of the thugs. "Who turned you, Roman? It's not the cops. Jackson would've told me."

Roman helped Madelyn to her feet. She felt lightheaded and sick to her stomach. She leaned into Roman for support.

"I'm not going to say anything until you let her go," Roman said.

Oleg snorted. "I'm going to ask you once more— who got you to plant this thing?"

Roman wrapped his arm around Madelyn's shoulder. "Let her go and I'll tell you everything. She's innocent, man. Just in the wrong place at the wrong time."

"Wrong place? Wrong time? Isn't that the truth. She's not leaving here, but I bet you'll talk to make her death quick and painless." Then to the thugs, he muttered, "Bring them into the office."

"No. No. No. Please, let me go," she begged. Like a mouthful of spoiled fruit, humiliation for having to plead left a rotten taste in her mouth. Yet what other choice did she have? She knew little of self-defense, and doubted that jabbing one of these men with her keys would do anything to change events. "I swear, I won't say anything."

"Go," said Oleg.

"I'm not going into that office," said Roman. "Neither is Madelyn."

His words gave her enough resolve to disregard Oleg's order.

Oleg hitched his chin to one of the thugs. He withdrew his gun and pressed the barrel into Madelyn's temple. The metal was cold and hard.

Oleg said, "I'm tired of playing games. If her well-being matters to you, tell me what I want to know and she'll die quickly. You have my word of honor."

The thug released the safety of his gun with a click that was deafening.

"No, no, no," she wept. There were so many things Madelyn had yet to do. She needed to finish med school. She needed to say goodbye to her parents. Her sister. "Please, Roman, help me."

"Okay." Roman held up his hands. "We'll nego-tiate."

"Call it what you want. Get into the room."

The barrel bore a hole into Madelyn's temple and she was shoved forward by the pressure of the gun.

A metal chair sat in the middle of the room. The thug pressed on her shoulder. "Sit."

Her knees buckled and she sank to the chair. Fear made her useless, paralyzing her mind, her spirit and her body.

For a single second Madelyn was five and stand-ing on the curb in front of her house, watching Ava run across the street as she headed to the park.

"Come on, Maddie," Ava called.

Madelyn hesitated and looked toward the house. Her mother wasn't there to either give her permis-sion or forbid that Madelyn leave the yard. Without another thought, she bolted into the usually quiet street. Suddenly, there was the blare of a horn. The grille of an old pickup truck filled her vision and she froze with fear.

Madelyn tumbled to the pavement, landing on her back. The pickup truck screeched to a halt, the bum-per well beyond where she'd been standing. Madelyn was in Ava's grasp. In that moment, she knew that her sister had saved her life.

Yet as she felt the cold steel of the gun against her skull, she knew there was nobody to save her this time.

Chapter 2

Roman didn't like the odds. Three armed men against one. A locked room with no chance of bringing in backup and top that off with a terrified woman, for whom he was now responsible. If he were a betting man, he'd place his money on Oleg Zavalov winning. Thank goodness Roman had never wagered in his life.

"One last time before I get medieval on your girl-friend," Oleg said. "Who do you work for?"

A fiery sense of self-loathing filled Roman. This whole situation was his fault. He should've marched Madelyn up the stairs as soon as she walked into Oleg's office, to hell with her stubbornness. Instead he had what? Flirted? It was an amateur move, but at the same time, a little of the world's ugliness had melted away during their exchange.

To top it all off, he was about to lose five months of work. And more than that, Oleg would know that he was being investigated and have time to dispose of any evidence. Roman opened his mouth, ready to confess all. He couldn't find the words.

What he could find was a lie. "I don't know what you have, Oleg. But it's not mine."

"It's an ELD, a bug, a listening device."

"How am I supposed to know about those things?" Roman asked, a little regretful that he couldn't claim his latest creation. "I'm just the bartender."

"I don't think you do. I think she does."

"But I don't," Madelyn said.

"If it wasn't you, why'd you run?"

Roman answered for her. "Because I'm standing at the top of the stairs and when I turn around, there's Serge and Anton with their guns. I told her to run. It's what you do when someone threatens to shoot."

Oleg's mouth hung open for a minute, then like it was controlled by a puppeteer's string, it snapped shut.

Fighting the urge to smile, Roman took in a deep breath. A pain shot through his side from a kick or punch he didn't recall receiving. Madelyn looked at him. She was beautiful in a delicate way. She wore a navy blazer and white T-shirt that fitted her pert breasts and trim waist perfectly. Her dark hair was cut short and her brown eyes were large. Her skin was creamy and smooth. To him, she looked perfect, almost magical, and he wished like hell that magic was real and she could simply disappear. Small gold hoops dangled from each ear and a gold chain hung around her neck. Funny how small details became important when you were standing next to the thin line that separated life from death.

Oleg tossed the ELD in the air and caught it. "There's one thing I do know, is that one of you two planted this bug. So, I'll ask again—how'd this get in my office?"

"I don't know," Roman said.

"What about you?" Oleg turned to Madelyn. "How'd this get in my office?"

Madelyn quietly wept and shook her head.

"Nothing to say?" Oleg leaned his hip onto the corner of his desk. "Maybe you need the right motivation to talk. Make her sorry, Serge."

Serge cracked his knuckles, a smile lifted the corners of his mouth. He brought back his arm and slammed his fist into Madelyn's face. She toppled from the chair. A bright red mark bloomed to life on her cheek.

To hell with the work or the loss of the investigation. Roman wouldn't let Oleg hurt Madelyn any more. Although if they made it out of this alive, Roman would take great pleasure in bringing Oleg Zavalov to justice. It wasn't professional anymore. It was personal.

"Okay, Okay." Roman held his palms up and

stepped between Serge and Madelyn. "I'll tell you everything."

"Everything?"

Roman swallowed. His side burned. "Yes."

A phone rang and Serge pulled a cell from his pocket. *"Da."*

While with Delta Force, Roman had studied over a dozen languages. He was fluent in Farsi, German, Spanish, French and Russian. Even if he hadn't, the single Russian word was easy to translate. *Yes.*

"Oleg." Serge held out the phone. *"Vy khotite, chtoby prinyat eto."* Oleg, *you want to take this.*

"Ne seychas," Oleg said. *Not now.*

"Seychas," Serge insisted. *"Eto moy dyadya Nikolay."*

Serge's uncle Nikolai was on the phone? Nikolai Mateev?

Oleg sat taller and reached for the phone. He met Roman's gaze and his eyes narrowed. Had Oleg guessed that Roman understood the short conversation? Roman looked away.

"Lock these two in the beer cooler," said Oleg, "but stand guard. We'll deal with them later."

Serge pulled Madelyn to her feet. Anton withdrew his gun and motioned to the door. "Go," he said.

Serge worked both locks on the outside of the beer cooler's thick, white door. Madelyn was shoved in first. She stumbled over the doorjamb and fell to the metal floor with a hollow *thump.* Roman calmly stepped inside and turned to face Serge—the man he now knew for sure to be Nikolai Mateev's great-nephew. "I'm going to get out of here and then, I'm going to kill you for hitting Madelyn."

"Is that a wager, you stupid American?" he asked in halting English.

"I never make bets. It's a pledge."

Serge snorted. "Your promises bore me."

The door slammed shut, leaving Roman and Madelyn in complete darkness.

Madelyn skidded across the cold metal floor and crashed into the wall. Every part of her body ached, throbbed or pained her. She didn't care. She fumbled with the purse's clasp and pulled out her phone. She hit the home button and the screen glowed.

"That won't work in here," Roman said. His voice came out of nowhere. "If it did, one of Oleg's men would've taken your phone before they threw us in."

She ignored him and dialed 9-1-1. The phone icon tumbled across the screen.

"We're underground. The walls are cinder block, which makes the signal weak at best. Then you throw in these." He wrapped his knuckles on the door. The metal walls echoed. "There's no way for a signal to get through."

She didn't listen, staring instead at the cartwheeling phone icon.

"Madelyn, it's not going to work."

Roman knelt next to her, light from the phone illuminated his face. His lip was split and, for a moment, she recalled the feel of his mouth on hers. Was that to be her final joy in life? A kiss from a stranger?

"How can you be so calm, while we're sitting here waiting to die?"

Roman gently rested his hand on her wrist. "We aren't going to die," he said.

"Yes, we are. Those men will be back. They said so."

"I don't care who's coming. I'm not going to let a turd like Oleg Zavalov end my life—yours, either. But to get out of here, I need you to work with me. Can you do that?"

The next call failed. It looked as though her only option was Roman. She took in a fortifying breath. "Okay, what do we do?"

"Bring your phone over here. I need a light on this lock."

Madelyn used the screen to light their way. He knelt before the door and she illuminated the catch.

"Do you have a credit card?"

"For what?"

"If the dead bolt isn't engaged, I can slip a credit card between the jamb and the door and disengage the first lock."

Madelyn's pulse began to race, but this time she felt hope and not dread. She reached into her purse and pulled out her wallet. The open end tipped over, scattering the contents of her handbag. Seeing the debris of her normal life on the floor brought tears to her eyes. The keys to her apartment and car. Her

ID for the University of Colorado Hospital. Lipstick. Nail clippers. Two peppermints and a lint-covered bobby pin.

Would she ever need any of it again?

"Here." She handed him a card and repositioned the phone to shine on Roman and the door.

He worked in silence for a moment before muttering a curse. "It was too much to hope that they'd be careless and not use both locks. I can open the bottom lock. To get out, I need to unlock the dead bolt, too."

"So that's it? We can't do anything else."

"I'm not giving up. Shine your phone on the walls, there has to be something we can use."

Madelyn illuminated the walls from right to left. She saw nothing helpful, but then again—she didn't know what he wanted to find.

"Bingo," said Roman.

Her sweep stopped and the light shone on a thermometer.

Roman pried the face of the thermostat free, exposing the guts of the device. "It's not as good as piano wire." He worked a thin piece of metal free. "But it'll do."

Holding it up to the light, Roman continued. "I need you to shine your phone's light on the door and keep your credit card steady at the same time."

She slipped her wallet back into the bag and knelt next to Roman. His body heat enveloped her, warming her, reassuring her that he would do everything possible to save both of their lives.

Roman reached for Madelyn. His hand was large, with smooth calluses, and strong. He led her fingers to the card. "Hold it steady, just like that."

She felt the tension in the thin plastic as it was held between the door and the jamb. "Got it," she said.

He regarded her. In the light of the phone, his green eyes blazed. She moved closer to him, his breath brushed over her cheek. Madelyn never used the word *brave* to describe herself, nor *adventurous*. Yet as Roman moved forward, erasing the space between them, Madelyn took the lead and placed her lips on his. "In case we don't make it out of here alive," she said.

"We'll make it." He turned back to the door.

She smiled, not daring to hope and yet not able to fathom what would happen to her if they didn't.

Roman's breath stilled, and Madelyn held her own. Even in the freezing cooler, sweat damped Roman's hair. He had a tattoo on his forearm. A screaming eagle with a banner in its talons.

"Hoc defendam," she said. "This we'll defend?"

"It's the army's motto."

He'd been in the military. It explained a little— like how he knew how to handle himself in a fight and maybe even how he'd learned how to pick a lock. What it didn't explain was why he was planting a listening device in Oleg's office and what he hoped to overhear. Before she had time to wonder anymore, the lock clicked.

"Got it," Roman said.

The door opened a fraction of an inch. Warm air and light leaked into the cooler. Madelyn didn't have time for the tears of relief she wanted to shed. Sitting back on her heels, she collected her belongings. After shoving everything into her purse, she rose to her feet.

Roman peered into the hallway. Madelyn, at his back, looked over his shoulder. The door to Oleg's office was closed. The man who'd been ordered to stand guard was nowhere in sight.

"There's a door at the end of the hall that leads to a set of stairs and then an alleyway. We're going out that way. Stay by my side and don't make a sound."

Madelyn held her breath and stepped into the hall. Roman carefully clicked the door shut behind them. Holding Roman's hand, she quietly moved down the corridor. The door at the end was locked, but an electronic keypad clung to the wall. She waited while Roman entered a set of four numbers, certain that the pounding of her heart would give them away.

Two things happened in the same instant. A light atop the gray, metal box changed from red to green. One of the thugs came out of an adjacent room.

"Chuto, chert voz mi, ty delayesh?"

Madelyn had no idea what he'd said, but then again, she didn't need to. The gun in his hand spoke volumes.

Glaring at Roman, Serge switched to English. "What the hell are you doing?"

One person. One gun. Roman's odds were getting better and better. He stepped in front of Madelyn, shielding her with his body. The need to protect her was more of an instinct than a thought and he held his hands up, as if he intended to surrender.

Wordlessly, Serge jerked the gun toward the cooler.

Roman nodded, hands still lifted, and moved from the door. His focus sharpened to a razor's edge. He kept his gaze connected with the thug's, yet his concentration was on Serge's hand, his arm, his gun.

Back to the wall, Roman inched toward the cooler—and Serge. Five feet away. Four feet. Three feet. Strike. Roman grabbed the gun's barrel and wrenched it to the side. He twisted the firearm toward Serge's thumb and at the same time, chopped down on the thug's wrist. Roman righted the firearm, placing Serge into his sights.

Not sure of his next best play, Roman paused. In Russian, he said, *"Opustoshit vashi karmany."* *Empty your pockets.*

Nikolai's nephew gave a wry smile and shook his head. *"Ty govorish' po-russki?"* *You speak Russian?*

"Da, chert voz' mi, teperi' opushoshit' vashi karmany." *Damn right, now empty your pockets.*

"Da, da, da," said Serge. He withdrew his cell phone, wallet and a package of cigarettes from his blazer. He tossed them on the floor. From the pocket of his slim trousers, he pulled out the set of keys and threw those into the pile, as well.

"Walk," Roman said, his voice little more than a whisper. "And if you make a sound I'll blow your brains all over this hallway."

Serge sauntered toward the cooler. He reached for the handle and then he swung out. Roman dodged back, but not far enough and the blow hit the gun's barrel, knocking it from Roman's grasp. The gun skittered down the hall, stopping next to where Madelyn huddled by the door. Roman wanted to tell her to run, but he could hear Oleg's voice behind his closed office door, which meant that Oleg would be able to hear into the hallway, as well.

Serge bolted forward. Roman held out his arm, catching the other man midchest with a clothesline and knocking him back. Roman pounced before Serge had a chance to rise. He drove his fist down again and again. Roman's arms ached, a stitch in his side burned and throbbed. His sweat-damp shirt clung to his torso like a second, gritty skin.

Nikolai's nephew held up his arms to block the blows. His hands and wrists took more punishment than his face. Serge brought up his legs, hooking them over Roman's shoulders. Shifting his weight, the thug knocked Roman onto his back. Then Serge crawled to stand and Roman grabbed him by the foot. He came down hard and Roman pressed down on his back. As Serge began to scream, Roman clamped his hand on the other man's mouth and nose. His arms swung out wildly with ineffectual punches. His hits slowed and then stopped altogether.

The body went limp. There was no breath. Roman felt for a pulse that he knew he'd never find.

"Damn it," he cursed.

In the silent hallway, he heard Madelyn's stifled sobs and Oleg's voice from behind the door. *"Konechon, Otets, ya ozhidal uvidet' vas poslezavtra."* *Of course, Father, I will see you here tomorrow.*

Otets. Father. Sire. It was a code name often used with Nikolai Mateev. Was the head of the Russian Mafia coming to Boulder? It was the information that Roman had been waiting five months to gather. He needed to contact the team from Rocky Mountain Justice right away, but first he had to hide Serge's body.

He grabbed all of Serge's personal effects and dropped everything, except for the keys to The Prow, on the dead man's chest. Roman opened the cooler door and then dragged the body inside. He locked both locks and returned to Madelyn.

"Is he…?" She hiccupped as tears ran down her face. "Is he dead?"

Neither of them had time to mourn. "It was him or us," he said as he entered the back door's code. The lock disengaged with a click and Roman pushed the door open. He peered outside and saw nothing more than a set of metal stairs ascending to the alley and the backside of a Dumpster.

He opened the door further and reached for Madelyn's hand. They'd done it. They'd escaped. But then from behind came an all-too-familiar voice. "Black!"

Oleg stood in the corridor. "Anton," he screamed. "Serge! After them."

Anton rushed out of the office.

"Get the car," Oleg said. "Chase them down."

Roman didn't wait to see if Anton followed the orders. He pushed Madelyn into the night and pulled the door shut. Gripping Madelyn's hand again, he sprinted up the stairs. His feet hit the pavement as a large raindrop fell on his forehead and the back door to The Prow burst open.

He held tight to Madelyn and willed his legs to move faster. The stitch in his side had returned, turning every breath into a fiery torture. He fixed his gaze on the intersecting street and ran faster still. Rain fell, wetting his skin and blurring his vision.

"My car's two blocks up and one over," Madelyn said, her voice breathless with exertion.

He liked that she was thinking. All they needed to do was outrun Oleg and Anton for three blocks. Or better yet, lose them. Roman pushed on. The end of the alley grew larger with each step. He ran through the intersection. On the other side, he kept close to the buildings and let the shadows hide his movements.

Still running, he began to scan the alleyway. The recessed doorway ahead was deep enough to surround them in complete darkness. Rudimentary, sure. But simple plans were often the best.

He ducked in and drew Madelyn in behind him. Together, they huddled in a corner. Her chest rose and fell with each labored breath. Her heartbeat resonated within his flesh. Maybe it was all those months of undercover work, but he was getting a little too used to holding her.

In the darkened alleyway, her skin took on a luminescent quality. Her lips turned a deep shade of burgundy, like a sultry and smoky wine. Her nose was small and straight and the hollow on her neck looked as if it had been meant to be kissed—by him. Next to her, Roman felt too large and at the same time, protective. It was because he blamed himself for getting her involved with Oleg.

Oleg. His footfalls echoed off the buildings while he ran past. The sound died away as he continued to run.

"Is he gone?" Madelyn whispered.

Roman held one finger to his lips. He peered down the alley, Oleg's retreating silhouette was nothing more than mist in the increasing rain.

"He's gone," Roman said. "Let's get out of here. It won't take long for him to figure out that we've given him the slip."

Together, they ran to Madelyn's car. The pace was slower, but still Roman ached. One block up and one block over, but to Roman it felt like miles.

"What is that thing? It looks like a toy."

"That," said Madelyn, "is my car."

"That thing?" The powder blue auto came up to his chest. He'd never fit inside, or at least he'd never be comfortable. "Does it have a motor?"

Madelyn opened the driver's side door. "If you want a ride, get in."

For Roman, many things had gone wrong over the last few hours. But having to fold himself into some kind of origami figure just to ride in this *car* might actually be the worst part.

Putting the gearshift into Drive, Madelyn pulled on to the deserted street. The road was dark, the streetlights all broken. Buildings, soaked and dripping, were covered with graffiti. Rain pelted the windshield.

"The nearest police precinct is on Canyon Boulevard. Go north seven blocks and then turn left," Roman said.

"The police," she breathed. Thank God. Soon this nightmare would be over. She thought of Jackson, the man who'd captured her and insisted he was a cop, but that couldn't have been true.

She accelerated, the world outside her window becoming a blur.

"Wow," Roman said. "The gerbil in your engine can run fast."

"I'll have you know that this car has a TwinPower turbo engine," she said. She wasn't really in a joking mood, but the teasing helped to release some of the tension she held in her shoulders.

"Me, I'm an American muscle car kind of guy. Give me a Ford Mustang or a Chevy Camaro any day. So, I don't even know what a TwinPower turbo engine means."

"It means that I feed the gerbil in my engine really well," she said.

He laughed and winced, gripping his side. "This is your turn," he said.

Madelyn eased around the corner and a tall building of glass and brick came into view. It sat behind a wide lawn. A sign, illuminated by a spotlight on the ground, read Boulder Police Department. Madelyn felt warm and exhausted, as if she'd been wrapped up in a blanket, fresh out of the dryer, on a snowy winter's night. She slowed as she neared the curb. The double doors of the police station opened and two men stepped out. Madelyn's heart ceased to beat. A pair of blue jeans and sweatshirt had been traded for a police uniform, but the face was the same.

"Jackson's here," she said. "I'd hoped he was lying about being a cop."

Heads ducked in the rain, the men strode down the walkway.

"Just drive away," said Roman. "We'll think of something else. Maybe we can keep watch and come back after he's gone."

Madelyn stomped on the accelerator and her car shot down the street. She headed up the block. The back of the car filled with light as another car approached fast from the rear.

Roman said, "Looks like we have company."

She stepped on the accelerator, urging her small

car to go faster. The other auto, a bigger sedan, gained more ground.

Turning in his seat, Roman said, "It's Anton."

Before she could ask how he knew, they were hit from behind. Madelyn's car lurched forward, skidding sideways on the wet pavement.

Roman watched Madelyn as she drove. Shoulders hunched forward, she gripped the steering wheel and stared wide-eyed at the road. The speedometer climbed. If only Jackson hadn't been at the police station, this whole episode would be over. But, now they were on the run again.

"We have to lose Anton," said Roman.

"Not a helpful suggestion," said Madelyn, "especially since I don't know this neighborhood."

He did. "There's an alleyway half a block up and on the left. Turn at the last minute and hopefully Anton will pass us by."

She nodded, her jaw tight.

Roman counted. "One. Two. Turn."

Madelyn whipped the steering wheel. The car hit the curb, sending them airborne. They landed and she aimed for the small alley. As he hoped, the other car didn't make the turn. "Turn right at the end of this alley and then take the next left." He gave her another half a dozen directions that led them down side streets and into another alley.

"Pull up behind this Dumpster and kill the lights."

Without comment, Madelyn followed Roman's

instructions and they sat silently in the darkened car. Rain pelted the windows and filled the tiny space with constant noise. Madelyn's breath came in short and ragged gasps. Even in the dim light, Roman could see her pulse thrumming at the base of her throat. Up until now, she'd been brave and levelheaded. But everyone had a limit for what they could endure. Had Madelyn reached hers?

"Look at me," he said.

Her head snapped to him, her eyes were wide.

"I need you to breathe."

"Breathe? I'm freaking out, here. There's no place for me to go. Nobody I can trust."

Roman knew that she hadn't meant to injure him with her words, but the fact that he hadn't earned her trust made his cheeks sting.

Yet, why did he care? What was it with his reaction to this woman?

"You can trust me," Roman said.

"Can I? I don't even know you."

Roman didn't dignify her comment with one of his own. Instead, he said the only thing that might help her gain control. "You're a doctor, right? Every day you face all sorts of distressing scenarios, but I bet you don't freak out—" he made air quotes "—with your patients."

"Of course not," she said. "I'm trained to handle a variety of medical emergencies."

"Well, I'm trained to handle this kind of emergency. So, whether you think that you can trust me or not, you can."

Madelyn exhaled fully. "Okay. What do we do next?"

"Anton's not going to give up. There's too much at stake," he said.

"Then we are going to die," Madelyn said. The resolve of her statement was a blade to the heart, the first tiny cut of a thousand.

Roman brought up a map of Boulder in his mind. "We'll only get one shot to shake Anton off our tail, but first, we have to find him and get him to chase us."

Madelyn took in a shaking breath. "I think I like staying hidden better."

He wanted to say something to give her courage or at least comfort, like a pep talk, but after months of living a lie, he'd forgotten how to be inspiring. "Can I drive?" he asked instead.

She hesitated. "I guess."

Roman glanced out the side window. The building next to them was so near that he couldn't open the passenger door.

Her gaze followed his. Roman turned to look at Madelyn. She gave a little shrug. "Sorry," she said. "I can move the car."

"Don't bother," said Roman. "We'll just trade places."

She moved to hover above him, his hands on her waist. Sure, they were being chased by a murderous gangster but the fact that her nice butt was right above his lap didn't escape Roman. And it wasn't simply her body that he appreciated, either. As far as working with a civilian—Madelyn Thompkins wasn't half bad.

He moved across the cramped console and into the ridiculously small seat. Every muscle in his abdomen ached. He found the lever that controlled distance from the steering wheel and eased back, the pain in his middle lessening. With the headlights still off, Roman maneuvered out of the alley. He pulled onto a deserted street. Ahead, he saw the black sedan driving slowly in the opposite direction.

"Buckle your seat belt." Roman dropped his foot on the gas. The little car shot forward with more force than he would have imagined. TwinPower turbo, indeed. He closed in on Anton. Bumper swiping bumper, he rocketed past in a deadly game of tag.

Anton followed, as Roman knew he would. Left. Right. Left and left again. Left again and another right. He headed south, toward the interstate entrance ramp nearest the warehouses on the outskirts of town.

Anton stayed close behind. Ahead, a light changed from green to yellow. It was exactly what Roman needed. He stepped on the gas, rocketing through the intersection as the light turned red. Anton followed. The blare of car horns trailing him like a ship's wake.

Roman's foot lifted from the gas as the interstate drew near.

Madelyn swiveled in her seat. The headlights from behind surrounded her in a golden halo. "He's gaining on us," she said.

He knew. He smiled. Wait. Wait. Wait. There was a hairbreadth between Anton's car and the one that Roman drove. The road began to travel upward, the incline leading to the interstate. Nose up, Roman jerked the steering wheel hard to the right, the side scraping on a concrete barrier as it pulled onto the adjacent service road. Anton sped past, his red tail-light glowing as he stepped on the brakes. From behind came the piercing scream of an air horn. A big rig, loaded with two trailers, lumbered up the entrance ramp—forcing Anton to drive on.

"He won't be able to get off until the next exit," Roman said, verbalizing the last bit of his plan. "That's five minutes from here, which means we have ten minutes to disappear."

Rain hit Oleg's face, mixing with his sweat and leaving him chilled. He stood at the end of the alleyway and looked left, then right, then left again. The street was empty. His pulse raced.

"They're gone," he said to nobody in particular. "Just disappeared…"

His phone rang and he pulled it from his coat pocket. Anton's name appeared on the screen and Oleg swiped the call open. "You better have good news for me," he said.

"Not so much," Anton said. "They tricked me into getting on the interstate."

Oleg ground his teeth together. "Tricked you?"

"I have a license plate, though. That should help, yes?"

"No, as a matter of fact, it won't help."

"Prosti," said Anton. *Sorry.*

"I'm not in the mood for your apologies. Just get your sorry butt back to the bar." Oleg ended the call with a stab of his finger and slid the phone back into his pocket.

Oleg was surrounded by idiots. The only one with half a brain was Roman. How had they gotten out of the beer cooler? Serge must have unlocked the door. But why? Oleg wasn't about to discover the truth while standing in a downpour with the stench of rotten cabbage thick in the damp night.

Turning on his heel, Oleg took a step. His foot landed in a shallow puddle. Cold water seeped into his shoe, turning his $1,200 designer loafers into garbage. Oleg clenched his teeth, biting off a string of curses. Once he caught Roman, the traitor and his little girlfriend, he was going to make them exquisitely sorry.

In the distance, lightning split the sky in two. A springtime thunderstorm in Boulder? For a city that saw sun more than three hundred and thirty days each year, a passing cloudburst was a rarity. But a full-blown rainstorm? Never. Yet here one was. It was almost as unbelievable as someone escaping from The Prow.

He quickened his pace. Roman's car, a crappy Pontiac from the 1970s, sat in front of the bar. The handle was stuck fast, but it was still here—which meant they'd gotten away in the girl's car. He thought of going directly to Roman's apartment, but discarded the idea as soon as it came. Roman's place was an obvious choice, and he knew that the bartender wasn't that stupid.

He needed time to regroup, but Oleg wasn't about to let himself be seen like this—wet, dirty and rumpled. He jogged around the corner and let himself in the back door. Dripping, he went to his office to dry off and come up with a plan.

Oleg jerked his desk drawers open and slammed them closed. No towel. No dry shirt. Not even a used tissue.

"Serge," he called out.

Never mind that the guy was the nephew of Nikolai Mateev. He was a moron, and in Oleg's opinion, he liked hurting people a little too much. Look at that chair in the middle of his office. It was bolted to the floor—done by Serge without asking for permission, never mind getting it—so he could tie adversaries to it and beat them bloody.

Oleg was supposed to be teaching Serge about business, and not just how to run a bar, either. Nikolai's great-nephew needed to learn how ill-gotten money could be infused into a legitimate business and make any drug profits seem legally gained. But it was clear that Serge had no interest in that kind of education. Hell, he'd barely learned any English. With him, it was all about the violence.

Using his shirt's damp sleeve, Oleg buffed his face dry. He slumped into his seat. The godfather of Russian organized crime was due in Boulder tomorrow evening. Then Serge would become Nikolai Mateev's problem, and Oleg expected a generous reward for all the housekeeping he'd done. Babysitting and laundering—money, of course.

And speaking of babysitting... "Serge!" he bellowed.

Nothing.

Oleg stood and slammed his seat beneath his desk. He stomped up the stairs and entered the bar. Rock music pulsed through the speakers, thrumming into the soles of Oleg's feet and pounding out the beat in his chest. As the night had grown late, more customers had arrived and crammed into the room. They stood three deep at the bar. Now working alone, the bar manager bounced back and forth, like a frenzied ping-pong ball. He expected to see Serge having a drink. Nothing. Nor was he in the back shooting pool.

"You seen Serge?" Oleg asked the bar manager.

The withered old man shook his head. "Not since he left with you."

Oleg nodded and returned to the basement. Not only was Serge an idiot, he was also proving to be a mystery. The stockroom door stood ajar and Oleg opened it slowly. Empty. But maybe Serge had just been there. Oleg returned to the office. Empty, as well.

That left one final option, and one that didn't amuse Oleg in the least. Obviously, Roman had convinced Serge to open the beer cooler. Then had he overpowered Serge, making him a prisoner in the cell he was supposed to be guarding?

One more day and no more Serge. For Oleg, it couldn't come soon enough. He used his keys on both locks and pulled the door open. Oleg stepped up to the threshold and stopped.

Serge, obviously dead, stared at the ceiling. His gaze was already milky.

Oleg began to tremble and it wasn't from the cold. He had let Serge die. Nikolai Mateev would see it no other way.

The only thing Oleg knew to do to save his life was to disappear. He hated leaving everything he'd built up from the ground. The bar. The drug trade. His car. His women. All of it would vanish, like a candle flame that had been snuffed out. From the pit of his soul, fury rose. Oleg's head throbbed. His shoulders ached. He drew back his foot and kicked Serge again and again and again.

As a small boy growing up outside of Fort Collins, Colorado, Oleg had spent hour upon hour in the company of his paternal grandmother. As she cooked, she told Oleg stories of their family. His favorite was how Oleg was a direct descendent of the Romanov czars. In another time, he would have been Count Oleg.

Because of those stories, Oleg had known he was destined for greatness. And this—taking care of Serge the Stupid, laundering money for the Russian mob—was to be his way. But Serge had been too moronic to stay alive and in death had ruined everything. Everything. Oleg brought down his heel on Serge's nose.

He wiped his sole on the back of Serge's jacket. His heel caught on something, and he worked it free. Attached was a lanyard with an ID card for the University of Colorado Hospital. The picture was of a petite brunette. Name: Madelyn Thompkins. The seed of a new plan took root in Oleg's mind, flowering into the only chance he had at saving his legacy and his life.

Certainly, Nikolai Mateev would be furious that his heir apparent had been killed. And while Serge could never be brought back to life, Oleg could make sure that a recompense was paid to the murderers— Roman and Madelyn. And look, the degenerates even beat poor Serge's corpse.

All Oleg needed now was to find Roman Black and Madelyn Thompkins. While he imagined that Roman knew enough to get out of town, Madelyn had ties that kept her in Boulder. Besides, if given a computer and ten minutes, Oleg would know everything there was about Madelyn's life—or what was left of it, that is.

* * *

"Slow down," Roman said to Madelyn. "It won't do us any good if we get pulled over by Jackson."

Madelyn licked her lips and nodded, letting up on the gas. After Roman had lost Anton, she'd taken back control of her car. She slowed down a little, the headlights shining on a puddle. An oily rainbow floated on the surface. She gripped the steering wheel tighter, it was the only thing that felt real.

Roman said, "We're alive and in one piece. Just remember that."

"Alive and one piece," she echoed.

"I need to get in touch with my employer in Denver. Can I use your phone?"

She pulled it from her purse and handed it over. Roman entered a number, the phone's volume so loud that Madelyn heard the ringing.

Voice mail picked up. "You've reached Ian Wallace. Leave your message at the sound of the beep and I'll return your call promptly." The accent was British and educated. It reminded Madelyn of a blindingly white shirt, freshly pressed.

"Ian, it's DeMarco. Big happenings but I don't want to get in to too many details on an unsecured phone. I'm on my way to you and will fill you in when I get there." Roman ended the call. "Thanks," he said.

On a night that had too many questions and not enough answers, Madelyn needed to know who she was with and why. "I thought Oleg said your name was Roman Black. Now you're DeMarco?"

"I've been working undercover for months." He handed her the phone. "My alias is Roman Black."

It seemed like the only answer he was willing to give and she set the phone on the console between the seats. He'd spoken about leaving Boulder. What was Madelyn supposed to do? Drive herself to another police precinct? She needed to report what happened, but without Roman?

Roman gripped her arm. "I need a favor. My car is parked in front of The Prow. I can't go back for obvious reasons. Can you drive me to Denver?"

She could, but to her the real question was, did she want to? Sure, she wanted to help, but she also just wanted to be safe. She stared forward, indecision a rock in her belly. Madelyn switched her gaze to Roman. His palm remained on her wrist. Sweat dotted his upper lip. His hand slipped away. A bloody streak stained her flesh.

"Roman. You're bleeding."

"What? No, I'm not..." He touched his side and brought his hand up to examine by the light of the dashboard. His fingertips were crimson and wet.

"I need to look at your abdomen. You're wounded," she said. Her medical training clicked into place like a puzzle piece, and Madelyn now had a clear picture of what needed to be done.

"Sure," said Roman.

Madelyn pulled next to the curb and turned on the

dome light. She reached around Roman and pulled up his soaked shirt. A neat furrow had been dug out of his skin. "You were grazed by the bullet, so there isn't any internal damage," she said. "But you'll need stitches."

"I can get those in Denver."

"Denver is thirty minutes away, even without bad weather. Don't be the hero. Let's get you to CU's hospital and you can make another call from there."

"I'm not waiting around all night in an emergency room. I need to get to Denver now."

Roman's lips were pale, a sure sign of blood loss. She didn't have time to argue. Madelyn reached into her purse for her badge from the University of Colorado Hospital. It was proof that she, and therefore he, would get into the hospital's trauma center upon arrival. Wallet. Lipstick. Apartment keys. Three quarters and a nickel. She looked again. And again. "Where is it?" Madelyn searched through the console. Nothing.

"Where is what?"

"My hospital ID. I always put it in my purse and now it's gone."

Then she remembered those harrowing few minutes in the beer cooler. She'd accidentally dumped the contents of her handbag and then hurriedly collected everything once the door had been unlocked. Had she been too hasty?

"The Prow?" Roman asked.

The sour taste of bile rose in the back of Madelyn's throat. "It has to be there."

"We have to get you out of Boulder."

"I can't abandon my life. I have rounds at the hospital, classes. Besides, you need to see a doctor."

"I thought you said that you were a doctor."

"I'm a medical school student."

"Can you sew me up?"

"If I had the proper equipment, of course."

"Then drive. I'll keep pressure on my wound and give you directions as we go. Get onto the interstate and head west."

"West? Why not south and toward Denver? I thought you wanted to talk to your employer?" Whoever that was. She turned off the dome light.

"We have to assume two things," Roman said.

"Yeah? What?"

"First, is that Oleg Zavalov will find your ID. Soon, he'll know everything about you. Anton already has the make and model of your car along with your license plate. It's only a matter of time before Oleg has your address. Then Oleg will get people, like Jackson, out looking for you in all the obvious places—your apartment, the hospital and even the interstate to Denver."

"That's not reassuring." Rain fell heavily, a seemingly solid wall and not thousands upon thousands of individual water molecules. The wet road reflected lights, creating a world of reality and a wavering mirror image in the water. Madelyn pulled away from the curb.

"I wish I had better news," Roman said. "Because the second thing we have to assume will be worse."

"How can it be worse than Oleg Zavalov knowing everything about me?"

"As long as Oleg is out there, your life is in danger."

Chapter 3

The desolate road followed the profile of the mountain and Madelyn steered into the curve. Rain beat down on the car, the *swish* of the windshield wipers echoing the beat of her heart. Roman sat silently in the seat next to her. He pressed the bullet wound at his side, but was still losing blood. He was weak and the pressure to his side was lessening, which allowed for further bleeding. More even than the blood loss, she worried about shock. To counteract that, she needed him to stay alert. "Where are we going?" she asked. Forcing him to think and talk was the best way to keep Roman awake.

"Someplace Oleg will never find us."

His cryptic answer brought up another set of problems. She'd been foolish to chase after her sister, even though The Prow was a public place. Now she was all but lost on a mountainous road and in the middle of a storm, no less. To make matters worse, her navigator was a man about whom she knew next to nothing.

"I'm trusting that you're on the right side of the law, but you've never really explained anything to me. What is it that you do, exactly?" Madelyn asked.

"Private security," he said. "I work for an outfit out of Denver called Rocky Mountain Justice. My most recent assignment was to collect evidence about Oleg Zavalov." His voice was hoarse and raspy.

"Private security?" Madelyn's gaze widened. "You mean...you're a mercenary?"

Roman stared at her. "If that's what you want to call it, fine. Do we have to talk about this now?" He looked at the blood seeping from the wound, and her eyes followed his movement.

"I don't like that you aren't getting checked out by a doctor."

"Aren't you a doctor?"

"As I've mentioned before, no. I'm a med school student." She continued, "Which means that I know enough to know that you need more help than I can give you."

"You'll have to do for now," said Roman. "Besides, I've been in worse shape than this and survived."

Madelyn wasn't sure what to make of his comment. Macho bravado? Or was he telling the truth—

had he been seriously injured before? For some reason, she thought that the second possibility was right. She turned her attention back to driving as a bank of fog rolled in, enveloping the world in a robe of gray and black, obscuring the road beyond. She slowed to a creeping pace.

"See that left up there?" Roman asked. "Take that."

Madelyn slowed even further and peered into the night. A dirt track wound up the side of a mountain, disappearing into oblivion. She stopped, her mouth went dry. This was bad. Very bad. Sure, Roman had been the only reason she escaped from The Prow and was alive now. And true, giving a ride to someone who happened to be running from the same madman as she was made sense. But this?

"Where does this road go?"

"It's a safe house owned by RMJ. It isn't used much, and as far as I can remember, there isn't much to it. But it'll hide you away for now. There's also a radio I can use to contact Denver."

The fog lifted, yet the conditions only improved a little. This far into the mountains the darkness was complete. Because of the higher elevation, rain now mixed with snow, decreasing visibility even more. The headlights spilled across the wet pavement and Madelyn couldn't help but wonder: *If I drive off this road, will I ever get back?*

At the same time, she realized another important truth. While she didn't know exactly what to expect from Roman DeMarco, she did know what fate awaited with Oleg Zavalov. She'd die a horrible death. Roman had kept her safe until now, so maybe she could trust him a little while longer.

She took the turn. Nose down, the undercarriage hit a rut and bounced upward. Engine whining, the car trudged up the mountain. The tires chewed through the muddy ground. The trail leveled off and they rumbled over a rickety wooden bridge. Even in the dark, the muddy water buffeting the bridge was visible.

Upward again, Roman turned to Madelyn. "It isn't too far now." He raised his voice to be heard over the wail of the engine. "Two miles from the bridge."

Her eyes darted to the instrument panel. The temperature gauge had climbed to the top. "Good," she said. "I'm not sure how much more of this road my car can handle."

As if she had just given the small car permission to give up, the engine coughed, shuddered and stopped.

She turned off the ignition and waited a moment before trying to start the car once more. It screeched with protest.

"The engine needs to cool," Roman said. "It'll take a few hours, maybe more. We can wait here, or walk. It's your choice."

Roman was hurt and needed medical attention, not a two-mile hike. Then again, she couldn't treat him in the car. Neither option was good.

"Let's walk, but only if you feel that you're able," she said.

"I'm able."

Roman opened the door and slipped into the storm. Immediately soaked by the rain, he folded his arms across his chest, trying to retain some of his warmth. It wouldn't work well, Madelyn knew. She got out of the car, feeling that—in the very least—she could share his misery.

The cold and wet took her breath away. Gooseflesh covered her arms. She took a step. The sodden ground crumbled underneath and she slipped. Roman was at her side. With his hand under her arm, he kept her from falling.

"Thanks," she said, his breath was warm on her wet flesh.

"You're sure you're okay?"

She gazed at him. Rain trickled from the stubble that clung to his cheeks and chin. Madelyn caught a drop on the tip of her finger. Roman moved closer. Never had she been more keenly aware of what the word *alive* meant. It was to drink in every experience, to embrace each moment and never allow fear to take away desires. Roman's body heat was now a flame that both drew Madelyn to the warmth and left her certain that she would be consumed by the fire.

Then again, hadn't she been burned before? Hadn't that been the turning point that made her decide that her studies and career were more important than a relationship?

She wiped her wet hand on the leg of her wetter jeans. "I'm sorry," she said. "I shouldn't have touched you. This whole night is the stuff of nightmares, I just wanted to make sure you were real."

That wasn't it at all. Madelyn's flesh had acted of its own accord, seeking out her deepest longing—propriety be damned.

Roman smiled, and she couldn't decide if he had believed her lie.

"Let's go," he said. At least he seemed willing to let the moment pass. "This hill isn't going to climb itself."

"And isn't that a shame," said Madelyn.

"I'm glad you have a sense of humor," he said with a small laugh. "Because you're right, tonight has been the stuff of nightmares. Only now, waking up won't solve anything."

They walked silently, neither bothering to waste breath on small talk. Yet, what else was there to say? Madelyn refused to ask how much farther, turning herself into a whiny two-year-old. At the same time, complaining held a certain appeal.

"See that tree?" Roman asked, just as Madelyn's resolve to not grumble began to weaken. "The safe house is just beyond."

There were too many trees to count, yet she narrowed her eyes and strained to see through the dark. Atop a rise, she made out the shape of a dwelling. Even from the muddy track, Madelyn could see it was little more than a single room and yet, it was the best sight she could hope for.

Roman limped ahead, his breathing labored. "Walls, roof, a fireplace. It even has a well for water."

"It's great." Madelyn hurried to catch up to Roman, anxious to feel warm, dry and safe. "Perfect, really."

Roman unlocked the front door and held it open for Madelyn. She crossed the threshold. The air was thick and musty, and the room black as tar, leaving her feeling as if she'd walked into a cobweb. Reflexively, she brushed the back of her neck.

"No electricity this far into the mountains." Roman's voice came from further into the room. A quick hiss was followed by a whiff of sulfur. A match's yellow spark sprang to life, illuminating Roman's face from below. His cupped hand kept the flame alive as he touched the fire to the wick of an oil lamp. Light spilled around the room as Roman replaced a fluted globe.

With light, Madelyn could see around the single room. A set of cabinets lined one wall, cut in half by a counter with a sink. A sofa and armchair sat in front of a stone fireplace. A large table filled with electronic equipment that she could hardly name, huddled in the far corner.

"The bathroom's back there," said Roman. He pointed to the other door. "There should be some dry clothes in the cabinets if you want to change."

Madelyn was about to accept the offer, when she looked back at Roman. His complexion was pale, almost ghostly. The lantern in his hand trembled and shadows danced. Even more than from an odd casting of the lantern's light and his injury, it was obvious to Madelyn that Roman was quickly becoming ill.

She moved to him. Taking the lantern, she set it on the table with the electronic equipment. Her fingertips brushed the back of his hand. His skin was cold. "I'm fine for now," she said. She took off her purse and tossed it next to the lantern. "It's you who needs to get out of your wet clothes and I need to stitch up your side."

"I told you before, I'm tough. All I need to do is get a fire started." He took a step and rocked back and forth, his footing unsure.

"You might be tough—" Madelyn looped her arm around his waist and led him to the sofa "—but you are also stubborn." A throw blanket hung over the back of the sofa and Madelyn draped it over Roman's shoulders.

"I'm going to lift your shirt and look at your wound," she said, preparing him to be touched and asking for permission at the same time.

"Go ahead."

Madelyn peeled the cloth from Roman's side and he grimaced. Bright red skin surrounded an inch-long darkened furrow in his flesh. Blood no longer seeped from the wound, but still the skin had not yet begun to knit back together. She sat back on her heels. "Do you have a first aid kit?"

"In the bathroom." He pushed to stand. The wound began weeping blood.

"Just stay here." Madelyn patted his knee. "I'll be back."

The bathroom was small. Just a sink and toilet alongside a set of shelves. A white metal case with a red cross emblazoned on the lid sat front and center on the first shelf. The offerings were basic, but serviceable. She returned to the living space, ready to work.

Roman stood over the electronic equipment, swaying like a drunk.

"What are you doing?"

"This radio has its own solar generator and I can't get it working."

"Don't worry about the radio. Sit back down."

"I need to get in contact with my employer. I have information that an international fugitive is expected in Boulder tomorrow. They need to know."

His mission sounded important, and yet he also needed medical attention. To put it off longer could have serious consequences. "Use my cell phone," she suggested.

"It doesn't have a connection out here," he said. "I tried."

She wasn't sure how upset she should be that he'd pawed through her things without asking. Yet, not much of what had happened tonight was nice or polite, so she let her anger go. "Let me get you patched up. You can fix the generator in a minute."

"I'll keep." He bent, examining a black, plastic box.

"No," said Madelyn. She reached for his hand and led him back to the sofa. "Sit." He remained standing. "Please," she added.

With a sigh, Roman sank down. Madelyn laid out all she needed—alcohol pad, sterile needle and thread, antibiotic ointment, gauze and tape. Roman sat, stone-faced, as she cleaned, stitched and bandaged the wound. She gathered all the used supplies and discarded wrappers. "You're all set," she said, and brushed her fingers over his arms. His skin was cool, cold really. She handed him the blanket. "I'll get the fire started, just point me in the direction of the woodpile."

Roman clutched the ends of the blanket together. His teeth chattered. "I can't let a lady get firewood. Just give me a minute. I'll be fine."

"It's okay to let me help you and I promise not to think less of you for accepting assistance."

He hesitated.

"The woodpile?" she asked.

"Around the left corner, about ten yards away," he said. "You can't miss it. There's also a flashlight in the cabinet under the sink. You'll want that, too."

Madelyn grabbed the flashlight and turned it on. The beam was weak, but enough that she should be able to see thirty feet in any direction. "Thanks," she said as she left the safety of the little cabin.

In the few minutes that they had been inside, the temperature had dropped. The rain had ceased, replaced with snow and ice. The wind blew, freezing Madelyn's damp clothes and hair. The woodpile was exactly where Roman had told her. Madelyn reached for a small log and her heart sank. The wood was wet, soaked through by the recent storm. They'd never get a fire started with this wood. At least not now. Disheartened, she quickly grabbed several small logs and one larger one. Balancing it all, she hurried back to the cabin.

"This has to dry before we can use it for a fire," she said as she made a pile next to the hearth.

Her comment went unanswered.

Brushing her hands on the seat of her jeans, Madelyn turned to Roman. He sat on the sofa. He no longer shivered. Far from feeling confident at the absence of trembling, Madelyn began to worry about hypothermia.

She bent to him, her face mere inches from his. His eyes were half-open. "Roman."

He started, his eyes opening wide for a fraction of a second before slowly closing again.

"Roman, I need you to look at me and focus."

He regarded her through slits.

She recognized all the signs of a body temperature dropped dangerously low—extreme drowsiness, confusion, loss of coordination.

"Roman, look at me." Madelyn held up the flashlight. "Take this from my hand."

Roman swung out, his swipe well short of where she held the flashlight.

Her clear diagnosis—hypothermia. His resistance

to the cold had been compromised by the trauma of being shot and the subsequent blood loss. If she didn't act soon Roman's pulse could slow so dramatically that he would go into cardiac arrest.

"Roman," she said as she stripped away the blanket. "You're suffering from hypothermia. I need to get you out of your clothes. They're wet and stealing your body's heat."

"Leave the shoes on."

Roman was far more confused than she guessed. His shirt was already off, so his pants needed to be removed next. Without question, Roman was a singularly fit man. His pecs were perfectly carved and led to a set of abs for which the term *six-pack* was created. His jeans hung low, the muscles between abdomen and pelvis a well-defined V, like an arrow pointing to his... Good heavens.

As she unbuckled his belt and undid the first button on his jeans, Madelyn paused and reminded herself that the man before her needed medical attention, and this was in no way a seduction on her part. Then the fact that she needed to give herself that reminder gave Madelyn even more pause, but she continued to undress Roman. She worked the jeans over his slim hips and pulled them down his legs.

He reached for her hands. "Stop," he said. His voice a hoarse whisper.

"I need to get you out of these wet things, Roman."

His head lolled to the side. Madelyn knelt before Roman and untied his shoe. She slipped it from his foot along with the sopping wet sock, and pulled the leg free of his pants. She untied the second shoe and likewise removed it. She stopped, immediately understanding the situation. Angry, red scar tissue covered his foot. Two of the toes were gone.

Madelyn cast her gaze to Roman. He watched her with red-rimmed eyes.

"You *have* been badly injured before," she said.

He nodded. "Afghanistan."

"I'm sorry."

"I didn't want you to know."

"It doesn't matter to me," she said.

"Because you're training to be a doctor."

"Because you are a brave man and nobody makes it away from life unscathed."

She worked the other leg out of his jeans and reached for the blanket. It was damp and would do him no good.

"Is there another blanket here?" she asked.

Roman lifted a leaden hand, pointing to the wall of cabinets. "Sleeping bag. End cubby."

The tall door resembled a food pantry, but Madelyn found that it had been retrofitted with shelves and a bar for hanging clothes. She found a sleeping bag on the top shelf and pulled it free.

It was filled with heavy down and most important— dry.

Madelyn returned to Roman. She lifted one foot at a time and placed them in the sleeping bag. Then she began to pull the bag up over his body. The shimmy and tug was very much like putting on a pair of pantyhose. At the same time, it was vastly different. One of her legs wasn't two hundred pounds of muscle. Once she had Roman fully ensconced in the sleeping bag, she maneuvered him so he was lying on the sofa.

"How do you feel now?"

He mumbled unintelligibly.

Madelyn didn't like the fact that he was semiconscious. Still, the human body was an amazing thing and soon he would start to retain body heat. She kept busy for a moment, laying Roman's wet things across the backs of chairs.

"Roman?"

No answer.

She reached into the sleeping bag and checked his pulse. It was too slow and his skin was still cold.

Without dry wood, Madelyn didn't have a way to heat up the cabin or provide Roman with a warn drink—two of the best ways to increase his body temperature. That left her with only one option.

She took off her blazer and set it aside. Thinking only of the medical necessity of her actions, Madelyn stripped down to her bra and panties. "Roman," she said, unsure if he could even hear her. "I'm going to get into the sleeping bag with you. My body heat will help you warm up."

She unzipped the bag just enough to get inside. Roman's flesh was cold and she was instantly chilled. She fought the urge to rub his skin, knowing that was one of the worst things to do to someone suffering from hypothermia.

He opened his eyes for a moment, a smile lingered on his lips. "What's a nice girl like you doing in a place like this?"

"Isn't that what you should've asked me at the bar?"

"I did, if I recall—just not with the cheesy pickup line."

"Yeah," she said. "I'm sorry for not listening."

"You were looking for your sister. You love her and want to make sure she's safe. I should've told you more. It's just that..."

His voice trailed off and his eyes slowly dropped closed. Madelyn's heart began to race. She wanted to know about her sister. More than that, she was worried that Roman was finally slipping into a catatonic state.

"It's just that what?" She touched his shoulder. To keep him conscious, she had to keep him alert. "You were saying something about Ava."

He swallowed—a good sign, medically speaking, but didn't open his eyes. "It's just that I didn't want to put you in danger. At the time, it seemed like a good plan..."

What kind of danger had Ava stumbled across this time? But more important, how much danger was Roman in now? "You have to keep talking to me, Roman." Silence. "Tell me about the time you served in Afghanistan. You were in the army, right? I remember your tattoo."

His lips moved, but he made no sound. Madelyn moved closer to him, even though her body was pressed into his, and placed her ear next to his mouth.

"My platoon was tasked with rescuing a group of soldiers…" His voice trailed off. Madelyn was about to shake Roman, when he began to speak again. This time, his voice was stronger. "Go in, get the good guys and leave—that was supposed to be our mission."

"And things didn't go as planned," she said.

"The intel we had wasn't as good as it needed to be, but Delta Force will never back down. We got all our troops out unharmed. I took a few rounds to the foot, minimal collateral damage if you think about it."

"It's only minor if it's not *your* foot."

"Two surgeries and this was the best they can do." He began to tremble. "Sorry," he said. "I'm still so cold."

"Don't apologize. Shivering is good. It means that your body is warming itself up, not shutting down."

"Thanks for all your help."

His breath washed over her neck and Madelyn instinctively melted into his form. In this light, his eyes looked hazel—green and brown and gold—like the forest in the fall. Then she reminded herself that Roman was her patient. Then again, he wasn't. His shivering lessened and his skin began to warm. Realizing that he wasn't under her medical care left Madelyn keenly aware of the fact that she lay next to him in her underwear and that he was in nothing more himself.

"I should get up," she said, "let you get some rest."

"Don't go. Not yet."

Rain, snow and ice pelted the window. The soft tapping was the only noise in the little cabin.

"Okay," she said.

"I'm glad you're here," he said.

The breath caught in her chest. Of course, there were many ways she could take his comment—from the personal to the professional—and she couldn't come up with an appropriate reply. What was Madelyn thinking? She wasn't a fool. There was unquestionably a seductive undertone to Roman's words. While she appreciated his appearance and his bravery, she knew nothing about the man. What if he had a girlfriend, or—dear God—a wife?

"You shouldn't be asking me to stay in this sleeping bag with you or telling me that you're glad I'm here."

"Why not? It's all the truth. I do want you to stay and I am glad that you're with me now."

"I don't know anything about you."

"What do you want to know?"

"Are you married?"

"Divorced."

"Do you have a girlfriend?" Madelyn asked.

"No."

"Liar."

"Why would I lie to you?"

"To keep me here, in the sleeping bag, with you."

"I thought you were sharing your body heat with me."

"I am." Madelyn corrected herself. "Was. You aren't suffering from hypothermia anymore."

"Are you sure? I could easily relapse."

Medically, he was right. It could take several hours for his internal temperature to regulate.

"Besides," he said, "I don't have a girlfriend, if that's what worries you."

"I find that hard to believe. You're a good-looking guy," she said.

"I've been working undercover for five months. In my experience, girls don't like being ignored for almost half of a year."

"No, they don't," she said, if only to fill the silence.

"What about you?" he asked.

"Me? No, I'm too busy for a relationship."

But it was more than that. Madelyn's last relationship had ended for that reason, but it was her ex's choice, not hers. She was too focused on her studies to have time for him. Eating alone and spending weekends alone was fine if you wanted to be alone, he had told her, but he expected a little more from his girlfriend. Yet, the rejections still clawed at her middle and while trying to soothe away the pain, she had adopted the position as both a mantra and armor.

"I refuse to get serious with anyone until after I graduate. No one is worth sacrificing my dreams," she said. Even in her own ears she heard the defiance in her voice. Would Roman guess that it was forced and that her heart had been broken already?

"And yet here you are in a sleeping bag with a strange man," he said.

She couldn't decide if he was being playful or not.

"With everything that's happened tonight, nothing is out of the ordinary."

And Roman definitely wasn't strange. He had broad shoulders and well-muscled arms. His legs were long and a sprinkling of dark hair covered his chest and tickled her flesh. The spicy scent of Roman hung in the air and teased her senses. She wanted to taste him again and see if his kisses burned. She stared at his mouth, his lips.

The silence became the unclaimed yearning that filled Madelyn. She feared that if left unchecked, she would dive headfirst into the emptiness and ecstasy, never bothering to first discover the depth.

"I can see that Oleg is a bad man," she said, shoveling noise into the chasm that held her desires. "What were you looking for?"

"My employer had intel that Oleg was involved with Russian organized crime and one of the largest heroin dealers in the world, Nikolai Mateev. I was trying to plant a bug in Oleg's office tonight."

Roman continued to speak, telling her that he had a specialty in electronic surveillance and that as soon as he had warmed up, he would contact RMJ and tell them that he had intel about Nikolai Mateev's upcoming arrival. He finished by saying, "They're dangerous men, all of them. I'm glad that I finally have some information that will lead to indictments, arrests, and, hopefully, convictions."

"My sister was in The Prow earlier tonight. She posted a picture on social media, that's why I came to the bar."

"I remember."

"And now she's involved with these men?"

"I wouldn't say involved."

"What would you call it, then?"

"She's a regular and it doesn't surprise me that she's been in rehab before. But she's not friendly with Oleg or any of his crew, if that's what worries you."

"At least she's alive. These past few months have been awful." She paused again, not sure if she should continue. Maybe it was the fact that it was completely silent, save for the rain and snow tapping on the window. So, if she spoke it was almost as if the words were only being said inside her head, where only Madelyn could judge. "Ava's in Boulder and hasn't called me. She knows I'm a student at CU medical school. Why would she ignore me? I love her and want to help her." Then in her mind, Madelyn asked the most important question, the one she dared not voice. *Is there something wrong with me? Is that why everyone leaves?*

"Maybe she's embarrassed to see you."

"Me?" Madelyn began to sweat. "I'm her sister, for goodness' sake."

"Once we get Oleg Zavalov sorted out, I'll help

you find Ava. I've gotten to know some of the other regulars. They'll know where she's staying."

"You would do that for Ava?"

"I'd do that for you."

Madelyn's breath caught in her chest. She gazed at Roman. He smiled and her heart fluttered.

"Roman," she whispered.

He wrapped his hands around Madelyn's waist and pulled her close. She tensed, her emotions at war. She wanted Roman's lips on hers and for his hands to touch and explore more than her side. At the same time, giving in to her needs felt reckless and wrong.

"You were pretty great tonight," he said. "Not many civilians could face the likes of Oleg Zavalov and keep it together like you did."

"I was pretty scared, if I recall."

"Me, too," he teased. "But my fears were on the inside. And you're a hell of a doc, too. The folks at Walter Reed Medical Center couldn't have done better."

"Aww," she joked, "now you're just making me blush."

"I'd like to do more than that." His voice was smoky and deep. He cupped her face and stroked her cheek with his thumb. "Competent, intelligent and beautiful—it's a rare combination. And one that I am a complete sucker for."

He was offering Madelyn the appreciation she craved—at least for the night. Yet, she never gave in to her impulses, hadn't since she was a kid. "I can't," she whispered. "You've been shot. It wouldn't be a good idea."

Roman lowered his lids. When he looked up again, his gaze was no longer on her face. "I get it," he said.

Madelyn was glad that Roman understood her motivations, because where he was concerned she hardly knew herself.

Oleg Zavalov sat on the sofa in Madelyn's darkened apartment. Anton, returned from his chase onto the interstate, had driven them there. The bodyguard paced, his hulking shadow slowly moved from one side of the room to the other.

"Sit down," Oleg snapped. "You're giving me a headache with that back and forth routine."

"You think she'll come back?" Anton asked. "We've been here for an hour."

And it had been another hour since Madelyn Thompkins had escaped from The Prow. Two hours gone. "I don't think she'll be back," he said.

Anton took a seat. "Maybe we should call Serge."

Oleg pictured Serge, his cloudy eyes staring at nothing. "Serge is minding the bar."

"But it was shut down when I got back," Anton said.

Oleg, to keep the body hidden, had closed early for the night. He wouldn't reopen until Serge could be removed from the beer cooler. He'd have to remember all his lies to keep them straight. "He's busy doing other things."

"Is Serge out looking for Roman and the girl?"

"What do you care? Are you suddenly the boss?"

"I was thinking," Anton said. His Russian accent was dark and heavy, like a tobacco stain on lace curtains.

"Don't think," Oleg snapped. Then again, if Oleg was stuck in this apartment it didn't mean someone else couldn't be his eyes and ears on the street. He took the phone from his pocket and pulled up the contact list. The call was answered on the first ring.

"You can't call me on this phone," Jackson whispered.

"I need you to do something for me."

"I can't now, I'm on duty."

"Do you really want to deny me a favor?"

Jackson sighed and Oleg waited while a muffled conversation took place on the other end of the call. "I needed to get away from my partner," he said when he returned to the phone. "What do you need?"

"For you to look for a car."

Jackson sighed again. "Fine. Give me the make, model and license plate."

Oleg asked Anton for the information, which was readily given and then he passed it on. "Once you find that car, stop it and call me."

"I can't pull someone over for no reason, much less detain them without cause."

"Find a reason," Oleg said.

"Yeah?" Jackson asked, "Who's this person to you?"

"The car belongs to Madelyn Thompkins. She's the girl you stopped from leaving The Prow tonight."

"And you want me to find the car she drove because…"

"Drives." Oleg corrected the cop. "She got away, along with my bartender."

A long line of profanity followed. Oleg waited for the swearing to subside. "I'll help you this time," said Jackson. "But after tonight I'm done. Got that?"

Jackson liked the drink and the women that Oleg provided. The threat was empty and he'd be back. "Of course," he said. "Call me if you find anything."

Oleg put the phone in his pocket and exhaled. He leaned back on the sofa and pressed the heels of his hands into his eyes until a kaleidoscope of colors swirled in his vision.

"Since you know what kind of car the girl drives, you can have Serge out looking for her, too," Anton said.

"What is it with you and Serge?" Oleg asked. He wondered if Anton was going to be the biggest problem in keeping Serge's death hidden until he could deliver the culprits to Nikolai. Or disappear.

Two hours gone and Oleg's only hope of finding Madelyn or Roman was a hesitant and crooked police officer. There had to be more. Oleg closed the drapes and turned on the lights. He already knew everything about the room. Sofa. Chair. T.V. Coffee table. Breakfast bar. Kitchen. But in the light, he saw things that he'd missed in the dark. Family pictures lined the walls and thick medical textbooks sat on the breakfast bar.

Anton lifted a photo in a silver frame from the wall. "I know her," he said.

Oleg took the photo. It was the picture of two young women at a picnic table. Smiling, both held barbecued ribs. Sticky, brown sauce covered their fingers. He recognized one of the girls as Madelyn Thompkins. Her hair was longer and she was younger—Oleg guessed that she was eighteen or nineteen years old—but without question, it was Madelyn. The other woman was older by a year or two, thinner. Her hair was also long, but not neatly kept. There were also similarities between the two women. The eyes and nose were the same, different lips, though. Without question, the women were close relatives—sisters most likely.

"You recognize her?" Oleg put his finger on the other woman's face.

"I've seen her at The Prow. What's her name? Anna. No, Ava. Yeah Ava. Don't have a last name."

"Ava Thompkins?"

"Could be."

"Can you find her?"

"Most likely. I think she stays at the abandoned house next to the bar."

"Good, let's get out of here and go back to The Prow. Then I want you to find Ava Thompkins and bring her to me." Finding Madelyn was like try-ing to catch a single fish in a vast ocean. The task was nearly impossible, unless he had the right bait. Nothing would be a better enticement than a way-ward sister.

"I'll call Serge. He could get her and she'll be waiting for us when we get back."

"Leave Serge out of this," Oleg said, now cer-tain that Anton was soon going to be a problem that needed to be dealt with.

Oleg turned off the light, making sure that every-thing in Madelyn's apartment was just as it had been when they arrived. He sat in the back of the car while Anton drove. Serge's death was nothing more than a minor stumble on an otherwise clear path to personal greatness. It was that bloodline connecting Oleg to royalty that urged him to create another empire. And though Oleg had been born in America, he still heard the call of Mother Russia like a winter wind whis-tling through the eaves of the Kremlin.

Chapter 4

The final remnants of sleep surrounded Roman. Even though he had yet to open his eyes, his abdomen burned. The pain came with an understanding that he'd been shot. His mind began to take inventory of his body but stopped as soon as it began. A woman's form was melded into his own and it wasn't just any woman, either. It was Madelyn Thompkins.

He hadn't lied to her last night when he told her that she was the total package, everything he appreciated in a woman. But he had to keep in mind that he didn't know much about her—and definitely didn't believe in anything as ridiculous as love at first sight. Hell, after dealing with his ex-wife, he hardly believed in love at all.

What was it about Madelyn that sent Roman's pulse racing and brought a smile to his lips? Her little jokes? Her ability to face her fears? Deep down, it was more than that and even as he smiled to himself, he knew that to let her distract him would be a mistake.

It brought back the magnitude of the information Roman possessed about Nikolai Mateev. It filled him with excitement. More even than when he received his appointment to West Point, or when he ran in the winning touchdown at the Army-Navy game. To have information about Nikolai Mateev, one of the world's biggest drug dealers, was unbelievable.

But good intel officer that he was, Roman had to wonder, why would Nikolai come to Colorado, and Boulder specifically? There were places where an international drug lord could happily escape scrutiny, but not in America.

Sure, Roman knew that he wanted to reconnect with his great-nephew. But why here?

Roman wasn't going to solve any problems lying in bed. But while he was here, Madelyn was very nice to hold.

Her skin was translucent, as if it had been wrought from porcelain. Her rosy cheeks looked as if they were painted by an artist's hand and her eyelashes were too thick and full to be real. But after seeing her in action, he knew she was far from a china doll that might break. He smoothed a lock of her hair back. Stealing a touch was wrong, but...

The sun had not yet broken over the mountain peaks and the sky was a soft gray, like the wings of a young hawk. Roman slipped from the sleeping bag and stood in the middle of the floor, naked except for his boxer shorts. Cold leached in from the wooden planks underfoot. His old foot injury burned with each step. He checked his jeans and T-shirt from last night—still damp.

At least RMJ stored several sets of clothes in the cabin. After all, it was a safe house, used in cases of extreme emergency, and had provisions to last twenty people for a week. After collecting a pair of camouflage pants, Henley shirt and a down vest, Roman snuck into the bathroom. His reflection was as bad as he imagined. A purple bruise surrounded one eye, his lip was split and his shoulder was scraped and raw. Aside from the bullet wound in his stomach, which hurt like hell, Roman had still gotten his butt kicked.

He'd heal, though. He always did.

After washing up and dressing—carefully, to avoid pulling at the bandages—he returned to the living room.

"Morning." Madelyn's voice was heavy with sleep and sexy, to boot. She lay on her side, her head cradled in the crook of her arm.

She was a woman who had awakened something more than desire in Roman. Something about her made him want to be…better. A better man. That notion terrified him more than a platoon from the

Taliban. Why was that? Had he become so used to playing the role of an uncaring bartender that it was who he had become? Or was the explanation far simpler—was Roman incapable of truly being the good guy anymore?

Kneeling at the fireplace, Roman arranged kindling and crumpled newspaper. Striking a match to the paper, he said, "Thanks for patching me up last night."

The flame consumed the old news and began to lick at the twigs. Roman balanced a few larger pieces of wood atop the whole pile, all the while knowing that he was doing more than building a fire—he was buying himself time.

"Things got pretty real last night," he said, immediately wishing he could take the words back and start over with something much more suave. "With Oleg and Serge and Anton."

"Yeah," said Madelyn. She continued, her words stretched out to a comic length. "Real crazy, that is."

Roman snorted a laugh. "Are you always ready to make a joke?"

"We're alive. Why wouldn't I be happy?"

He turned to answer her and his mind froze as he took her in. Her hair was tousled. Her lips were a deep shade of a dark and sultry wine, and her eyes were the color of dark chocolate. Good Lord, it was like she reminded him of a dessert or something. Roman didn't care. Where Madelyn Thompkins was concerned, he was starving.

"You hungry?" he asked as he rose to his feet. "I

can't promise you anything other than food that's edible."

"Edible food is my favorite," she said.

Roman could come to like her corny sense of humor. He moved to the kitchen.

"I guess I should get dressed first." Madelyn sat up on the sofa with the sleeping bag clutched to her chest. He immediately understood that she wanted privacy.

"The clothes from last night are still damp," he said and withdrew a set of sweats from the cabinet, setting them on the table. "I need to grab some more wood and I'll give you a minute to get dressed."

"Thanks," she called out as he let the door shut behind him.

He decided not to worry about fixing the radio. The repairs would use up more time than they were worth. After breakfast, they'd walk back to Madelyn's car and get off the mountain. There was a cell tower near the road. By seven o'clock, he'd be in touch with RMJ and well before the rush hour had ended, they'd be in Denver. After that, Madelyn would be placed in protective custody and before noon, Oleg would be arrested. Not a bad day's work.

But once they'd made it back to Denver, Roman would have to let Madelyn go.

Like he ever had the ability to lay claim to her in the first place. At one time, he had been what that ladies called a "real catch." Star football player at West Point. Delta Force officer. Smart. Not bad looking. And then he went to Afghanistan and all that changed.

Madelyn was too kind to want someone as jaded as Roman and that truth pissed him off.

With wood in his arms, Roman kicked open the front door. Madelyn knelt in front of the fire. With her hands in flame-retardant gloves, she arranged a campfire cauldron over the blaze.

While he was outside, Madelyn had donned the sweatshirt he'd left her. She swam in the fabric and yet the swath of gray terry only made her look more feminine. Her legs were bare—strong and supple. She smiled when he walked through the door and Roman's mouth went dry.

"I poked around a little," she said. "I hope you don't mind. You had some oatmeal and dried fruit in a plastic container. I figured that should make us a decent breakfast."

Smart, tough, brave, beautiful, loyal—and she could cook over an open fire. Roman shut the door with his shoulder and dropped the wood on the floor. With an audible exhale, he wished that for one minute Madelyn would quit being perfect and start acting like a fallible human. "Sounds great," he said.

She drew her brows together. "You sound gruff. Have I done something to offend you?"

Had he? He hadn't meant to. "This is all great, really. I guess I'm sorer than I thought."

Madelyn rose to her feet. "I can examine your stitches, make sure there isn't an infection."

"I'm good," he mumbled, the image of Madelyn's palms splayed against his abdomen branded on his brain. He needed to stop these ridiculous fantasies before he forgot the mission completely.

He brushed past her and peered into the pot. The water had yet to boil and oats floated on the surface. He rummaged through a drawer and pulled out a long-handled spoon and stirred. "You should've waited for the water to boil before adding anything. Now the oatmeal will be lumpy."

"Okay." Her voice was small but steely, like a needle-pointed sword. "Are you sure I haven't offended you in some way, all of a sudden?"

"No," he said, setting the spoon aside.

He knew what he was doing. In being unpleasant, Roman wanted to create a gulf between him and Madelyn. It's not that he didn't like her. He did. Then again, that was the problem. "I'm just upset about how things went down at The Prow."

She looked away. "I'm sorry that I messed up your surveillance."

The fact that she apologized left Roman feeling like a heel. Now it was his turn to look away. What had she done to him to bring up all these emotions? Maybe it was the fact that she was perfect and Roman was far from it.

Oleg Zavalov sat at the bar and sipped a cup of bitter coffee. The sun had just risen and his eyes burned from lack of sleep. An all-nighter, and no Ava Thompkins. Yet.

Anton stood near the front door. With a phone to his ear, he nodded eagerly as if the other person could see him. He ended the call. "We have her," he said, slipping the phone into an interior jacket pocket. "The Thompkins girl."

Oleg's morning had just improved. "Which one?"

"Ava."

Madelyn would have been better, but with one he hoped to get the other. "Where is she?"

"She'll be here in a few minutes."

"You did well, Anton. I think you have real potential."

"Thank you," he said. Anton's accent thickened with the words.

A soft knock sounded at the front door fifteen minutes later. Oleg walked across the room to answer. While waiting, Oleg had taken time to clean up—wash his face, brush his teeth. His hair was slicked back with gel; a look he knew the ladies liked. Since Ava would be easier to deal with flattered and bribed than if she were forced to acquiesce, his jacket pocket was heavy with a gift he was prepared to offer her.

Oleg pulled the door open, a smile on his face. "Come in," he said as he stepped aside.

Ava cast a wide-eyed and wary glance around the room. Her shoulder-length hair was stringy and dull with dirt and sweat. Sores covered her face and a stained T-shirt hung on her frame. The shadow of her sharp collarbone was unmistakable beneath the threadbare fabric. As different as she was from Madelyn, the familial resemblance was also there. The same nose, eyes, coloring of skin and hair.

She stepped into the room and Oleg caught Ava's scent: stale body odor, vodka and the metallic undercurrent of fear. Oleg could see that she was smart enough to fear him.

"Come," he said, gesturing to a table set for two, and chivalrously pulled out a chair. "I'm happy you could join me for breakfast. I hope my invitation wasn't too inconvenient."

She pulled the loosened collar of her shirt together. "No, it wasn't inconvenient, not at all."

"Sit," he said again.

She looked over her shoulder once and then sat, perched on the edge of the chair.

"I hope you're hungry," he said, taking his own seat. "The kitchen is preparing us something special."

Anton exited the kitchen with serving trays balanced on both arms. They were laden with plates of bacon, eggs and toast, along with a carafe of coffee, mugs and glasses of orange juice. The nutty aroma of the coffee and the salty-sweet scent of the bacon filled the room. Oleg's stomach contracted painfully, reminding him that he had missed not only sleep over the past several hours, but food, as well. Anton wordlessly served and disappeared back into the kitchen.

Ava picked up the fork and regarded it as if it were something completely new to her. She scooped up one bite of eggs, then hunkered in front of her plate like a mongrel at a dish. It was almost enough to make him lose his appetite.

"You must be curious why I asked you here this morning," he said.

Ava scooped eggs into her mouth with a piece of toast and shrugged. "A little," she said.

"Your sister came here looking for you."

Ava stopped midchew. "Madelyn was here?"

"She wants to help you."

"That sounds about right." Ava pushed the now-empty plate away. "Is that what all this is about? You turning me over to my do-good, perfect sister?"

Oleg took a bite of his bacon and let this newest bit of information settle. Ava held more than a little hostility toward her sister. But was the animosity so deep that she would knowingly betray her own family?

"I hate to tell you this, but your sister isn't all that perfect. She left with one of my bartenders last night."

Ava stared at his full plate, her eyes wide. She twisted the collar of her shirt around two fingers. "That doesn't sound like Madelyn. She's too clean-cut. Besides, why do you care who your bartender hooks up with?"

"People change, yes? Or worse yet, they only allow us to see a mask—who they want us to believe them to be, not who they are."

He took another bite of bacon. Ava trained her gaze on the food in his hand. The bacon turned rubbery in his mouth as he recalled his grandmother's stories of the hungry Russian winters. And then there were the days when his mother was busy working two jobs and Babushka wouldn't feed Oleg, just so he understood how badly starvation hurt.

As those memories came to Oleg, he knew that his grandmother had been right. His suffering had made him stronger. But for now, he was benevolent. He pushed the plate toward Ava. "Help yourself," he said.

Ava reached for Oleg's breakfast. She ate all the food, until nothing remained except crumbs. She collected those with her dirty fingers and licked them away, as well. She pushed the plate back to the center of the table as he sat and silently watched her. "Thanks for the food. But what do you want? I don't think it's just to tell me that Miss Perfect likes to get busy now and again, because that's got little to do with me and nothing to do with you."

Oleg leaned forward. "I need to find your sister, that's what it has to do with me. I need your help, that's what it has to do with you."

"People always think that because someone *uses*, that their brain is fried. Or that they were stupid to begin with." She twirled her fork as she spoke and Oleg wondered if this was a speech she gave often. "I graduated top of my class in high school and I know how to do math. Something here isn't adding up and I'm not helping you until I understand."

"You know Roman, the bartender?"

"The big guy?"

"Yeah, him. He's been stealing from the till. I didn't have proof until last night. But before I could confront him, he left with your sister. I can't find him, but maybe your sister knows where he's gone." Oleg hadn't prepared the lie beforehand, but even he found it to be wholly believable.

"And you want me to do what?"

"Text her and ask her to meet you somewhere."

"Here?"

"No." Oleg spoke too quickly and with more force than he intended. "I don't want to spook Roman if they're together."

"Maybe the house where I've been staying."

"That would work, sure."

"You know." Ava leaned forward, propping her elbows on the table. "I came to Boulder months ago with a guy. He split, but I haven't contacted my sister. There's a reason. I don't want to see her and have her tell me about rehab or any of that crap."

"What's it going to cost me for you to get in touch with your sister?"

"I need some medicine to help me feel better."

Oleg produced ten plastic bags, no bigger than a child's finger, filled with white powdered heroin. He threw the bundle on the table and the baggies fanned out. Ava reached for them. Oleg dropped his hand down on the table, like a wall of flesh. "Text your sister and get her to meet you. Once she's on her way, you can have everything."

Ava reached into the back pocket of her jeans and produced a phone. She fumbled with the keys, speaking as she typed. "I need help. Come and get me." Then she rattled off a nearby address, one that Oleg knew belonged to a low-level dealer.

A text like that was certain to get an immediate reply. "Go ahead," he said. "Send it."

Ava's eyes twitched from the screen of her phone to the baggies on the table and back again. "She's not answering." Ava typed into the phone again and hit Send. Then again. And again. "I'm not sure where she is…"

Why would she know? Ava told him they hadn't seen each other in months or been close in years. "Do you have the right number?"

"This has been her number since high school." Ava held up her phone, showing Oleg the screen along with the 307 Wyoming area code. The contact was listed as belonging to a Maddie, along with a picture of Madelyn Thompkins in a marching band uniform. Oleg mentally repeated the number, memorizing it quickly. He scooted a baggie toward Ava. She tried to lift it, but he still held it with his finger. "You call me the minute you hear from your sister and then the rest is yours."

"I'll call you," she said, her eyes shining with a

hungry glint again. This time, Oleg knew the pangs had nothing to do with food. "I promise."

"You better keep your promise, Ava. I'm a good friend to have but a bastard of an enemy. You understand?"

She tugged at the drug-filled baggie. "I understand," she said.

Oleg lifted his finger and swept the rest of the bundles into his hand Anton reappeared and lifted Ava from her seat, leading her to the door. Soon she'd be back at the house and incapacitated. That was fine with Oleg.

He took a sip of the coffee, now lukewarm, and congratulated himself. By this time tomorrow, Madelyn would be dead. With any luck, Roman would be, as well. For now, Oleg could put this behind him and focus on what was truly important—a visit from Nikolai Mateev.

Madelyn slipped the long strap of her purse across her chest and tucked her shirt and blazer under her arm. The sweatpants Roman had offered were too big, so she donned her own jeans and shoes, along with the borrowed sweatshirt.

She stepped out of the little cabin. A large yellow sun hung low in a cloudless sky of bright blue. The sun and sky were deceptive and the air still bit with frosty teeth.

A shot came from behind.

In the split second she had to think, Madelyn pictured Oleg Zavalov hidden behind a tree with a gun. Instinctively she ducked and turned to the sound.

Roman stood on the porch, the noise nothing more than the crack of wood on wood as the door had slammed closed.

"You scared me," Madelyn said as she stood.

Roman grunted. "Sorry," he said, in a way that made Madelyn feel as if he were anything but.

What were she and this mysterious man, anyhow? Right now, it was easier for her to categorize what they weren't. They weren't friends, though she sensed that he was a likable guy. They weren't lovers, though Roman had a sexy, rough appeal that was more than apparent to Madelyn, and they had kissed. Nor were they doctor and patient, if only because Madelyn wasn't a doctor yet, and Roman hadn't really sought her out for treatment.

Without speaking, they fell into stride next to each other and headed down the same bumpy road they had climbed the night before. The ground underfoot was frozen, and Madelyn's ballet flats offered little support. Still, she trudged on, her quadriceps engaged and burning.

The pitch increased and she held out an arm to keep her balance. It wasn't enough. Her footing gave. She pitched backward, her stomach lurching. Roman's arm slipped around her waist, keeping her upright. He held her tightly, her back pressed to his chest. His strong arm rested under her breasts. Madelyn's nipples grew hard as her mind placed his exploring hands all over her flesh.

She breathed deeply to calm her racing pulse. It didn't work. Roman's exotically spicy scent mingled with the tang of the surrounding woods and Madelyn's heart raced even more. He leaned into her, his breath rushing over her shoulder, his hand spread across her middle. His fingertip grazed the waist of her pants. *Lower*, she wanted to beg. *Move your hand lower and conjure all those wicked spells that make me a woman and you a man.*

Then she remembered what they weren't and her spine went rigid. The clothes she forgot that she had been carrying lay in a heap by her feet. "Thanks for catching me," she said. Wiggling from his grasp, she bent to retrieve her discarded outfit.

"Just be more careful," Roman said as he stepped away. "I don't want to waste time dealing with your twisted ankle."

Madelyn sucked in a breath and gaped.

"You think you're the only one who's smart enough to treat an injury?" He lobbed the insult-infused question over his shoulder as he started down the road.

She swayed, tingling with the numbness of disbelief. "I never said I was smarter than you."

"You didn't have to *say* anything."

Roman's long legs carried him farther and farther away. To catch up, and keep up, Madelyn walked in double time. She reached for his shoulder and pulled him to a stop. "That's not fair," she said. "I only wanted to help you last night."

"I don't need to be saved," he said.

"Don't worry. I won't help again." Madelyn, determined to have the last word and the first step, started down the trail again. This time, Roman lagged behind. For the next half of an hour, neither spoke.

When they finally reached her car, Madelyn got behind the wheel without a word. Still maintaining the silence, Roman folded himself into the passenger seat. She eased the car around and drove down the hill. Her chassis shimmied and the engine whined. She didn't know much about cars, but she knew enough to know that both problems would be expensive to fix. Although that was a problem for another day. Oleg Zavalov was still out there, still deadly and still looking for her. Her savior had turned curmudgeon.

Following the face of the mountain, the road rose and the car crested a hill. Madelyn looked down and slammed on the brakes. The little wooden bridge they'd crossed the night before was gone. Brown muddy water swirled and foamed. It filled the creek bed and lapped at the side of the road. A chunk of dirt crumbled into the water.

Roman cursed under his breath. "The storm must've washed away the bridge. See if you have any cellular coverage."

Madelyn dug through her bag and withdrew her

phone. She hit the home button, but the screen remained black. "It's dead."

"Do you have a charger in the car?"

Madelyn shook her head. "I never keep one in my car, only at my apartment."

"And I didn't bother getting my phone from The Prow last night."

"What do we do now?" Madelyn asked.

"We don't have any choice besides go back to the cabin. The radio I spoke about last night can be fixed, so I'll get to work on that. It shouldn't be too much longer before we can call out."

"We could cross the stream on foot," Madelyn suggested.

Roman scratched his chin. "It's an option," he said, "but not a great one. More than last night's storm, the winter snows are melting. It's created more runoff than this little streambed can handle. Crossing would be risky," Roman said. "Besides, once we get across, we have to hike to the road and hope we can hitch a ride to civilization. I say we go back and fix the radio."

Madelyn didn't care for the plan. Admittedly, she didn't have a better alternative. At least they were talking again. The hurt-filled silence had bothered her more than she would have guessed. She turned around, her little car chugging up the hill. The engine's whine increased to a screech. The car shuddered, and then fell silent and still. She tried the ignition again. Nothing.

"Your car wasn't designed for this kind of driving," Roman said. "Must be that the gerbil gave up."

Madelyn gave a little laugh to cover up the tears she wanted to cry. "Poor fella."

"I know a little about motors," he said, "but with all new cars, the engine is more of a computer than gears and pistons, so I'm no help."

"I guess we have to walk from here," she said as she opened the door and stepped into the cold morning. Like her feet were encased in concrete, disappointment pulled Madelyn down. How could she help her sister if she was stuck in the middle of nowhere?

At the same time, this reprieve left her alone with Roman DeMarco, a man who left her breathless with desire and at the same time—so mad that she could spit. Yet, she couldn't help but wonder if Roman's injury or his time in the army had anything to do with his rapidly changing moods.

She decided that must be the case and then began to wonder what she might be able to do to help him heal…

A stabbing pain filled Roman's temple. It wasn't from an injury of the body, but rather the psyche. He'd been rude to Madelyn for no reason other than to keep her from being nice to him. The plan was solid when he thought they'd only spend the next hour or two together. Now, they were stuck in each other's company for who knew how long. And if they were going to get off this mountain, Roman would need Madelyn's help. More than that, he couldn't concentrate on fixing the radio if her enmity were like a third person in the room.

"My ex-wife always said that I saw apologizing as being weak."

"It's an interesting theory. What do you think?"

"That's a great question—one that a shrink might ask," he said. "I'm actually not trying to get all personal, I was just trying to create a segue for saying I'm sorry about being a jerk."

"Apology accepted."

"So, we're good?"

"Of course," she said. She smiled and Roman's chest tightened. He'd almost forgotten that the feeling existed, but he knew it well—or used to know it.

Satisfaction. The act of making Madelyn Thompkins smile brought Roman happiness.

A clear blue sky created a backdrop for the craggy mountain in the distance. He stared at the dark peaks, where heaven bent down to embrace the earth.

"It's quite a view," Roman said, as they crested a rise.

Madelyn came up from behind, her breathing labored. "It is beautiful," she said.

"We can rest a minute," Roman said. "The cabin will be there when we get back."

"I'm fine. Besides, you have to contact your employer." With a deep inhale, she strode on.

Roman reached for her, his fingertips brushing her shoulder. "A little rest won't hurt anything."

She looked at his hand and he let it cascade down her arm. Madelyn returned her gaze to Roman's face. Something was drawing him to Madelyn, the connection growing greater the more he was around her. For Roman, the experience was brand-new and at the same time, it felt as old as the hills upon which they stood. He stepped toward her.

Reaching up, Roman cupped her cheek. She leaned into his touch. He bent to her and placed his mouth on hers. She was soft and warm. He pulled her close, hardly believing that he was standing on a mountain, kissing this woman. She sighed, and her lips parted. Roman pulled her closer as his tongue slid into her mouth. She met his kiss and shivered with desire. In the distance, a blue jay cried.

His arms encircled her waist and he felt a deep-seated need to protect her, no matter the cost. It wasn't a thought as much as a code in his DNA. She wrapped her arms around his neck, pulled him to her. Their mouths met, tongues danced, arms intertwined.

He began to think that maybe a life of contentment could be his. Then he had to wonder, yet again, what this woman was to him that he was daring to think such dangerous thoughts. And more important, when did he become such an optimist?

The pessimistic side of Roman's nature—the one that knew best—whispered in his ear that Madelyn had been perfectly clear; she didn't want a relationship and if Roman tried to change her mind, he was only wasting his time.

And men like Roman weren't meant for anything long term—except loneliness. His life so far had proven that theory.

And still, Madelyn's arms were the best place he knew.

She released her grip a little and Roman knew that the moment, as perfect as it had been, was over. His hands still rested on her hips. "That was nice," he said.

"Nice? I think that's the understatement of the year," she said.

"Stupendous, then. Amazing. Angels wept."

"Now you're just being silly."

Roman held his pointer and middle fingers up-right. "I am not, Scout's honor."

"Oh yeah, I forgot. Mr. Eagle Scout, right?"

Roman let go of Madelyn's waist, leaving one hand at the small of her back. He began walking again, leading the way through the wilderness. "I really was an Eagle Scout."

Chapter 5

Madelyn walked in silence the rest of the way to the cabin. The scent of wood smoke from their earlier fire hung in the air and the snug cabin was still warm. Within a few minutes, Roman had stoked another fire.

"I'm going to see if I can get the radio and generator working and contact with RMJ."

"And Ava?"

"I'll ask them to start looking."

Madelyn wanted more, but wasn't sure what to demand.

Roman took a seat at the table. The black box with knobs and dials sat in front of him. Yards of white and black cord snaked across the surface. At his feet sat an open toolbox. "Is there anyone else you want me to get in touch with?" he asked.

Was there? She wasn't scheduled at the hospital for three more days. Would any friends call? And if she didn't call back, would her lack of a response cause them to worry? She called her parents once a week, and they wouldn't expect to hear from her until the weekend.

"I guess not," she said.

Roman turned back to the radio, her answer all but forgotten.

Madelyn opened several cabinets until she found what she was looking for—a pot, two mismatched mugs, and a tin box filled with tea. It was a mundane task, but Madelyn liked the pause from the tumultuous past few hours. Actually, the simple act of making tea was a welcome break in her otherwise hectic life. How long had it been since she'd taken a day off? Weeks? More like months.

She wanted to be a doctor more than anything in the world, but sometimes the sacrifices seemed extreme— like now. Resting for a day shouldn't only happen if hiding from a murderous gangster in the mountains.

Madelyn knew that there was more to her busy schedule than simply wanting to do well. It kept her from being alone—or rather, lonely. It was in those moments when she had nothing but time that she questioned if she were somehow flawed.

Funny—until now Madelyn hadn't wondered once

if she helped enough people would she somehow earn the right to some happiness—and she knew why.

It was Roman.

More than keeping her safe, he had kept her company, and that truth scared her more than a Russian with a gun.

The water began to boil and she filled both cups. "Do you take cream or sugar in your tea?" she asked.

Roman turned to her. He'd unscrewed the back of the radio, exposing the wires and circuitry. "Neither," he said, reaching for the cup. He took a sip and set it aside. "We have more problems than the generator. See this?" He held up end of an exposed of a wire. "It's been chewed through by something—a mouse most likely."

"What can I do to help?"

"Not much, unless you're an electrician."

"Nope, sorry."

"I didn't think so, but with you—heck it was worth asking."

Roman set his screwdriver aside and reached his arms overhead. His tattoo of the screaming eagle clutching the Latin motto danced seductively over the muscles as they flexed and lengthened. Fine hairs grew at the nape of his neck. She longed to touch him and see how his flesh felt under her fingers.

"It'll take about two hours for the generator to store enough power to make a call," he continued. His words drew her from her reverie and she blushed.

Roman turned to her and smiled. There was a

dimple on his cheek she hadn't noticed before. Her face warmed even more.

Madelyn was at a loss for words, but felt she should say something. "You were great in the fight last night at the bar." She exhaled and rubbed the side of her head in the exact place the barrel had pressed into her skull. "Especially how you took the gun from Serge."

Serge. Just saying his name felt wrong, dishonorable. The man had died so Madelyn could escape.

But still, she had to admit to herself that any killing left her unsettled. Especially when Madelyn admitted to herself that she was truly happy that Serge was dead. It wasn't that she blamed or judged Roman for his actions. It's just that she knew which side she was on in the struggle of life versus death.

Roman shrugged. "I did what needed doing. We obviously didn't have a lot of options."

"I was terrified last night. Once that man pointed a gun at my head, fear took over and I could no longer make my own decisions, just follow his orders."

"In a moment like that, you're preserving your own life. You did the right thing in listening."

"You fought them."

"I was fighting for you."

"Me? Why risk your life to save mine?"

"Because it's the right thing to do," he said.

"Because you're brave, and nothing frightens you."

Roman took another sip of tea and set his cup

aside. He moved from the table and took a seat on the sofa next to Madelyn. He took her hand in his. "I was scared, too. Being brave isn't the absence of fear, it's taking action even though you are afraid."

"Then I'm not brave."

"You are." He twined his fingers through hers. "You came to The Prow looking for your sister. The Prow's a rough place. It took a good bit of courage to do that."

"Yeah, but Ava's my sister and it doesn't matter what she's done—it's what she needs. Besides, we grew up together and shared all our secrets. Without her, how much of my childhood would disappear? How much of me will I lose?"

Oleg sat in his office, lines of code filling his computer screen. His head pounded and his vision was blurry. "Hurry up," he growled at the computer.

He sat back and closed his eyes. Even his mind was filled with blackness and row after row of pixelated dots. He'd been wrong to trust Ava or Jackson. It was almost ten o'clock in the morning and he hadn't heard from either one. It left Oleg with no one on whom he could rely beyond himself, so he spent the past two hours typing and searching.

"Oleg? You asleep?"

Oleg opened his eyes, Anton stood in the doorway, holding the jamb.

"And if I had been, then I wouldn't be anymore."

"It's Serge," Anton continued, his English halting and heavily accented. "I have heard nothing from him."

Oleg's heart slowed the span of one beat. His jaw tensed. "He's busy. I told you that."

"I know, it is that…" He paused and rolled his hand, searching for a word.

Serge was Nikolai's nephew, sent a year ago to the US to avoid pending criminal charges in Russia. His buddy Anton had tagged along. Oleg had accepted Anton as part of the trade, but with Serge's body still in the cooler, Oleg considered the deal to be null and void. It left him wondering what to do with Anton.

"He's fine," Oleg said. "You have my word on that."

The other man remained at the door and didn't show signs of leaving. "You have another problem?" Oleg asked.

"No," said Anton. "No problem."

"Good. Get back to work."

"And do what?"

The code quit running across the screen and the monitor went black. Oleg leaned forward, his eyes no longer fatigued. A road map appeared on the screen. Pulsating green dots represented cell phone towers appeared. Yes! He'd done it—he'd hacked into the cellular network and could now track Madelyn Thompkins via her cell phone.

"And do what?" Anton asked again.

"What?" Oleg didn't bother to look up.

"You told me to work. And do what?"

Oleg entered Madelyn's cell phone number. A bar appeared at the bottom of the screen, diagonal lines filled the first quarter. *Searching. Searching. Searching.* He glanced up. Anton remained at the door. "I don't know. Just find something to keep yourself busy."

Oleg returned his attention to the computer. He tapped his foot. He leaned forward, chin resting on his knuckles. He leaned back, head cradled in his hands. Half of the bar was filled. *Searching. Searching.*

"O, Bozhe." Dear God.

Anton's voice, hollow and horrified, came from the corridor.

Oleg's feet turned to ice. He knew what Anton had found.

Withdrawing a handgun from his desk drawer, Oleg slipped the barrel into the waistband of his pants at the small of his back and wandered to the beer cooler. Anton knelt on the floor next to the open door of the beer cooler. His skin was pale. His hands trembled.

"Vy." You. Anton rose to his feet, and turned on Oleg. Much taller and stronger than Oleg, Anton scowled as he towered over him. *"Vy yego ubili. On byl mertv techeinye neskol kikh chasov." You killed him. He's been dead for hours.*

"Bud' blagorazumen," Oleg said. *Be reasonable.*

"Razumno?" Reasonable? Anton shoved Oleg, sending him into the wall. *"Nikolay budet slyshat' ob etom." Nikolai will hear of this.*

"Nikolay?" Without thought, Oleg pulled the gun from his waistband and fired once. His ears rang, deafened to all other sounds. The metallic scent of cordite hung in the air and a puff of smoke drifted lazily toward the ceiling. He would have found the scene strangely beautiful—the silence and the smoke—except for Anton, who lay on the floor, gripping his own neck. Blood leaked between his fingers, surging from a stream to a trickle with each beat of his weakening heart.

He returned to his office and sat at the desk. A map appeared on the screen. A pulsating red dot, for the last *ping* from Madelyn's phone, along with a time—11:47 p.m.—and GPS coordinates. He hit several more keys and pulled up satellite imagery, glimpsing a county road that wound through the mountains. Expanding the view even further, he brought up a clearer picture that included a dirt trail disappearing into a dense forest.

He memorized the GPS coordinates before powering down his computer. Pocketing his keys, he left the office and locked the door. The stench of blood, coppery and thick, hung in the air. He turned to look at Anton's body, growing cold in death.

Even though Oleg had ordered The Prow closed until further notice, it wouldn't do to leave a corpse in the hall. He hefted the body around until the door could shut. A cell phone clattered from Anton's other hand. The screen was illuminated, the phone still open.

011-7-208. Anton had begun to dial out of the US and into Moscow, but had died before completing the call.

Oleg searched Serge's pocket and found his phone. There were twenty missed calls; all from Anton, except one. It originated from a Moscow-based number, as well.

Nikolai?

Oleg would be foolish to assume anything else.

He stepped into the hall and slammed the cooler door shut. Blood spray arched across the walls. A sticky pool of maroon and black covered the floor near where Oleg stood. Bright red streaks leading from where the body had been dragged were still wet. He ignored it all and strode toward the door.

It was far-fetched to think that Madelyn Thompkins had taken a dirt road leading to nowhere, and therefore out of cell tower range, yet it was the only option that provided Oleg with any action to take. And if he was wrong? Well, then he was lost in more ways than one.

Roman sat at the worktable, tools and wires scattered around. He'd rewired the radio and, in theory, it should work. Yet, for all his technical expertise, he couldn't get a message out. Frustration, a hot poker to his gut, bubbled up in a curse.

"What's the matter?" Madelyn sat on the sofa, her legs tucked beneath her shapely rear.

"This thing." He swept his hand toward the generator. "I'm worried that the solar battery has been drained too long to hold a charge. No generator means no radio."

"And that means you can't get in touch with your boss," Madelyn offered. Then she added, "But you left a message last night that something big had happened and you were on your way to Denver. By now, they know you never made it, and must be looking for you. Would they come here?"

RMJ operated more than a dozen safe houses around the state. But they'd look other places first. "Maybe," he said. "Eventually."

He moved the generator to another spot in the sun. The needle jerked as the battery began to retain power. "I'll give it another half of an hour," he said.

"So what do we do while we wait?" she asked.

Several thoughts, all pretty immoral, came to mind before Roman settled on one that was far too chaste for his liking.

Standing, he held his hand out to Madelyn. She reached for him and he liked the way her palm felt next to his. "I figure I can teach you a few moves that'll help if you get into another situation. The first lesson of self-defense is that your goal is to get away, not to incapacitate a combatant."

"Combatant? I'm not a soldier and I'm definitely not at war."

"Wanna bet? You are unquestionably engaged in a battle against Oleg Zavalov."

"I'm never going back to The Prow."

"Just humor me, then. Because I don't trust him not to come after you."

She hesitated, then straightened her sweatshirt. "What first?"

"Try to take me down," Roman said.

"I'm not comfortable with this."

"You aren't supposed to be comfortable, Madelyn. You're supposed to put me on the floor. Look at the tea. You could throw the liquid in my face, then bash me in the head with the cup. It wouldn't knock me out, but it would make my ears buzz and take me a few seconds to shake off, which is all the time you need to run."

"It would also have me treating you for burns."

The tea wasn't even tepid, much less hot. "Knowing how to defend oneself is the first step in accepting that one isn't always safe. It leaves a person weak and exposed at first. But until they face their fears, they can never achieve more."

"Why are you so determined to talk about me getting attacked again? Just the idea that I'll freeze again is horrifying."

"The hardest thing I've ever done," he said, now terrified of sharing his lowest moment and being vulnerable himself, "was getting out of the bed after my surgeries had failed. I was given a medical release from the military along with a pension that covered my living expenses. Yet, I'd wanted to serve in the army ever since I was a kid. Soldiering wasn't a job for me—it was my way of life."

He paused. His memories of his room at the VA Eastern Colorado Jewell Clinic were as fresh today as they had been six years ago. Three chairs of molded plastic lined the wall next to his bed. The seats created a hideous rainbow: mustard yellow, pumpkin orange and—his least favorite—bile green. The days dragged on, one miserable minute connected to the next.

"My last tour had been in Afghanistan as an intel officer with Delta Force. I'd picked up chatter about a missing platoon being held in some nearby caves. We used the cover of darkness to get close. Everything went as planned until the very end. We were spotted. Shots were fired. Several of their guys were killed. We only had one casualty—me and my foot. I know I've told you that part before, but not what happened next." He drew in a deep breath, willing himself to stay calm, not to let the anger he'd fought for years bubble to the surface again. "I get home and was lauded as a hero and given an honorable discharge in the same breath."

"What'd you do?"

He shook his head. "There was nothing for me to do," he said. "My mangled foot was in traction, held right in my line of sight. So, I lay in bed and loathed fate for screwing me over. That hate overflowed into the rest of my life. My marriage had been built on a fault line. You know—it's all his fault, it's all her fault."

"Oh, Roman." She took his hand. This time, he let her hold him.

"Anyway," he continued, "my crappy attitude didn't help. When my ex asked for divorce, I signed— thankful she wouldn't come for her daily pity visit.

"Then one day, when I was at my lowest, I got a visitor. He was a Brit—clean-shaven, pin-striped suit, yellow tie, pocket square. So very proper he looked like he'd stepped out of a business meeting at Barclays bank or something. He was MI5, retired, and had gotten a hold of my personnel file. He was starting a new private security firm and wanted to build a team."

"Rocky Mountain Justice," Madelyn murmured.

Roman nodded. "I recall his exact words, 'You're the bloke for me.'"

"Bloke? Did he really say 'bloke'?"

"Scout's honor."

"You must have agreed, because you're working with RMJ now."

"I did and I am," Roman said. "But not right away. In agreeing to take the job—to help start a firm—I had to let go of my loathing for myself and my sit- uation. There is a great deal of comfort in being a victim. But I had to get past that. Once I did, I was free." He paused, realizing that he hadn't really let go of all his self-hatred. He'd gone to work, but hadn't let anyone get close to him since being discharged from the army.

Thankful Madelyn hadn't picked up on his

thoughts and asked him to share, he continued. "Along the same lines, there's a great deal of comfort in learning how to defend yourself, because once you learn—you are responsible for your own safety. It's like me with RMJ. In agreeing to take the job, I was responsible for my own future."

Madelyn licked her lips—just a flash of her pink tongue on her red mouth. The gesture was simple and, at the same time, sexy as hell. It drew him deep into his fantasies. His mouth on hers. His hands on her body. Her breath on his neck, as he slid inside of her. He let the image consume him.

"So, you're saying…" her words pulled Roman out of the illusion, slamming him back into reality with such force that his head hurt "…that knowing some self-defense is accepting that bad things are possible and that's frightening?"

"Isn't it?"

She shrugged. He knew she agreed, but he didn't push her to say anything.

"What should I do first? And I'm not throwing tea on you." She picked up her cup and took a sip.

"Don't worry about hurting the other person. That's the point. Go for the balls, trust me—it hurts like hell to get kicked there. The eyes, the larynx, the nose. And put all your force into your punch." He swung his arm out to the side, in demonstration. "Don't just use the strength in your arm. Bring it up from your shoulder, your waist, your leg."

Madelyn copied his move.

Roman held up his palms. "Hit me," he said.

Madelyn threw out a punch. "That hurt."

Roman nodded. "Keep your fist tight and wrist strong. That'll help in a real way." Palms lifted, he said, "Try again, and remember—bring your power up from your feet." He touched his finger to her bare knuckles.

Madelyn threw a hit and then another.

"Lesson two—don't simply hit here." He touched his palm. "Go through the palm. But aim here." He pointed to a spot six inches behind his hand. Both hands up, he said, "Try again. Fist tight. Wrist strong. Aim behind the target."

She struck.

Roman shook out his hand. "Not bad at all. I'd say you've learned to deliver an effective punch."

"What if someone comes after me with a gun again?" Madelyn asked. "Even if I hit him, he can still shoot."

Roman looked around and grabbed a wooden spoon. He held it out to Madelyn. "This will be our gun. Take it and point it at me."

Roman handed it over. Madelyn squinted down the "stock," lining Roman up with the wooden barrel. Then Roman was the one pointing it at her.

"Do that again," she said. "But slower this time."

Roman held out the spoon to her. "Point it at me."

Madelyn followed the direction.

"Now I'm going to lift my palms, like I'm surrendering, but what I'm really doing is getting my hands free. I'm going to grab the barrel." He did and was pleased to see that she nodded at his instructions. "Then I'm going to turn it into your thumb and bring my other hand down on your wrist." He followed through with the movements and once again, the spoon was in his hand and pointing at Madelyn. "The momentum of the twist will almost pull the gun around."

"Let me try," said Madelyn. "Lift. Twist. Strike. Aim." The movements were slow but at the end, she was the one with the spoon.

"Good," said Roman. "Just keep practicing until you aren't performing separate steps, but it comes to you as a single motion."

They ran through the drill again and again. Lift. Twist. Strike. Aim. Lift. Twist. Strike. Aim. Madelyn's movements became fluid, like a dance, and she could take the spoon-gun from Roman with the same confidence as he from her.

"Feel better?" asked Roman.

"I do," she said, her voice and eyes bright.

Roman did, as well. He wanted to do everything he could to protect Madelyn, not just from Oleg—but always. And even though they'd part ways soon, his training would remain with her forever.

"Another tough situation is if you're ever grabbed from behind. I'm going to grab you." Roman snaked an arm around Madelyn's throat. "Move so that my elbow is in front of your throat. It gives you room to breathe. Now squeeze your fingers into the bend, pull out and then drop all your body weight to the ground."

Madelyn did as she was told, ending up on her knees. He offered her his hand to help her up. Once she was standing, he said, "Next time you'll be ready and land on your feet."

She turned her back to him. "Let's try again."

Roman reached around her neck, pressing his arm into her throat. As he had instructed, she moved so that her throat was at his elbow. She gripped his arm and pulled away. At the same moment, she dropped down. Her elbow slammed into Roman's side. A blinding, white light exploded in his vision as pain surged up and down his side. He sucked in a breath.

"Roman." Madelyn gripped his arm and led him to the sofa. "I'm so sorry."

"It's okay, I should've been more careful."

"Can I make sure that none of the stitches have torn?"

"Sure," he said, his teeth gritted. Waves of pain radiated from his side. Madelyn lifted his shirt and prodded the wound. Her touch was soft and cool and soothing.

"The stitches have held," she said. Her hand remained on his side.

The small cabin suddenly felt massive, and even though she was right beside him, Madelyn was too far away. He wanted to be closer to her, needed to feel the whisper of her breath on his naked skin. He groaned.

"Does this hurt?" she asked.

"Not in the least," he said, not caring that his statement was brazen and the sexual invitation was unmistakable.

She lifted her eyes. Their gazes held. She bit her lip. He bent to her, sucking her lips free. She sighed and gripped his shoulders, pressing her body into his. Their forms melded, their mouths together, their tongues entangled. In an instant, Roman needed to lose himself inside of Madelyn and the friction that brought complete bliss.

His fingers found their way under the fabric of her sweatshirt. Her skin was warm, smooth and oh so soft. His hand traveled upward, up her torso, her rib cage, until he found her breast. He cupped her, rubbing his thumb over her already hard nipple. She gave a sigh of desire. He wondered if she wanted him as much as he wanted her.

"Madelyn," he breathed between kisses. "I want you. Tell me that you want me, too."

His mouth found the hollow of her throat.

"Roman," she said. Her voice was weak. "We need to talk."

We need to talk. That was never a good sign. He took a deep breath, recovering, and placed his chin on top of her head. Her hair was soft.

"I like you," she said, "but this is going too fast, don't you think?"

He let her go and moved away. For Madelyn, Roman was a protector and defender—a person needed in the moment, but not after. For him, Madelyn represented everything that was good in the world.

Of course, she didn't want anything beyond a couple of kisses—he'd been a fool to hope for more.

"No pressure from me."

She bit her bottom lip and he refused to kiss it free, although he was sorely tempted to.

"It wouldn't be fair for me to lead you on. I am so busy with school and completely committed to my studies that I really make a lousy girlfriend. What's worse, I don't want to change."

He nodded and stood. After walking to the table. He picked up the generator, but saw nothing.

"I've offended you," she said. "I'm sorry."

"No need to apologize. You don't have to worry about me."

"Just living through last night was momentous and I don't want to start some kind of fling or relationship on this wave of emotion, just because I'm happy to be alive. It wouldn't be fair to either of us and might confuse things."

He met her gaze. "I'm not confused."

"It's a proven fact that the brain's chemistry changes after intercourse to create an artificial affection between partners. Mother Nature's way to keep couples together in case of a pregnancy."

The silence that followed was absolute, as if Madelyn's words had flushed away every sound. There was nothing artificial about the way he felt. Damn it, he hadn't even liked someone in years. But that barely mattered if she didn't return his affections.

The fire in the hearth popped and cracked, and then Roman remembered to breathe. He'd be damned if he was going to allow her to use her medical training to negate his feelings. His ego couldn't stand the sucker punch. "So," he said, changing the subject completely. "Ravioli or soup? We still have to wait on the generator, so we might as well eat."

She approached him slowly. "I'm sorry if I upset you. I guess I'm not very good at this relationship thing. I've been too focused on my studies for a long time and whenever I try, it never ends well."

That seemed to be her go-to excuse, although he imagined there was also a measure of truth.

"It's not that I don't date," she continued. "I do. It's just not that often and I typically wait weeks before…getting intimate."

His lips quirked in a sardonic grin. "No artificial affections, right?"

"Something like that."

"Like I said, you don't have to worry. I'm not offended." Even he heard the bite in his words and didn't believe them. "You never told me what you want? Soup or ravioli? I have cans of both."

"It doesn't matter," she said. "I'm not that hungry."

Roman ignored the regret in her voice. "Ravioli, it is."

Chapter 6

Madelyn undressed and stood in the middle of the
small bathroom with a pot of hot water perched on
the edge of the sink. Steam rolled upward, condens-
ing into a mist on the small mirror. The linoleum
underfoot was cold and she shivered. She knew that
the gooseflesh climbing her skin had nothing to do
with the chill in the air. It was Roman who had her
trembling with desire.

He was undeniably sexy. His appeal was rough—
tougher than the usual academic types that she went
for—and who usually dumped her when she refused
to put them before her work.

She skimmed her hands over her flesh, traveling
the same path she knew his would take. She held one

breast, her own thumb strumming over her nipple. Her other hand traveled to the juncture between her thighs and she ran her finger over the top of her sex, slick and swollen, with want. Her own touch was a paltry substitute for Roman's.

And at the same time, a small voice in the back of her mind asked, *Why?* Why stand alone in the cold, when she could be warmed in Roman's embrace? Why reject affection and spurn her longing, when she could lose herself in his arms? Why hold on to an antiquated truth that she would be a bad person for giving in to her nature, when all she wanted was to be free of expectations—at least for now?

Her hands fell still and silent, and hung at her sides. She opened the door, just a crack, and peered out. Roman stood at the window, his head rested upon the sill, his gaze trained to the woods that surrounded them. He'd pushed up his sleeves and his tattoo peaked out from the cuff.

Hoc defendam. This we'll defend. For Roman, it was more than a motto, it was a way of life. And she should know. He promised to keep her safe, and he had. It was his courage and conviction that drew Madelyn to him as much as his physique. Which said a lot, because his body really was a work of art.

His form was bathed with golden sunlight, making him look like a god come to earth. Her own Apollo, ready to carry her into the heavens. His pants hung low on his waist and hugged his well-formed rear. His broad shoulders looked as if they could bear the weight of the world. While she was sure that his strong arms would carry her to the edge of ecstasy—and beyond.

At the same time, Madelyn recognized that there was more to her attraction than a chemical reaction—pheromones and high levels of serotonin. It was him—the way he willingly sacrificed himself to ensure her safety. That he cared for her well-being, even if it was to offer her clean clothes and a bowl of canned pasta. All that, and rock-hard abs. She was a fool not to take him as her lover.

But if she did, then what?

Madelyn let the door fall closed and leaned into the wood, unsure whether she should congratulate herself for restraint or curse her cowardice.

Was her drive causing her to let life glide by? No. She hadn't entered medical school blindly. She understood what the sacrifices—both financial and personal—required. Yet, she was not on campus. There was nothing to study, nothing to save for right now. In fact, no one would ever need to know if she let go, just this once.

It wasn't as if she were a virgin. Roman would be far from her first lover. Well, not too far from her first lover...

She took a breath, looked at her reflection and opened the door. Roman remained by the window. He turned as the door creaked on its hinges. His eyes opened wide, his mouth slipping into an O of surprise. Both lasted the briefest of seconds before his gaze darkened and his lips set into a thin line. Did he disapprove? There was no way she had mistaken the passion in their kisses and his desire for more. As she stood there, Madelyn felt more exposed than simply being naked.

"You're beautiful," he said, "but I don't want you to feel pressured into doing anything. You said no—I get it."

"If you haven't noticed, I don't allow myself to be pressured into things I don't want to do, even if they're for my own good. Besides," she dared to joke as she crossed her legs and folded her arms across her chest, "maybe a roll in the hay is just what the doctor ordered after last night."

"I want to make love to you, Madelyn. I like you—that's why I want to be with *you*. Not because I need consoling or we're stuck in the mountains without any internet access."

"Am I being chastised?" she asked.

"Warned."

"If you've changed your mind, I can just finish washing up..."

Before she could step back into the bathroom, Roman crossed the floor. His lips, heated and ardent, were on hers. His hands blazed a path across her skin. She met his kiss with her own, their tongues joined, dancing and fighting for submission and control. She fumbled with the buttons of his shirt and peeled the garment over his head.

His pecs were strong and his abdomen rippled

with muscles. A dark sprinkling of hair covered his chest and ringed his nipples. Meeting in the middle, his chest hair traveled in a straight line down to the waist of his low-hung camouflage pants.

She wrapped her arms around his neck, rising on tiptoe to deepen the kiss. He was hard, the fly of his pants pressed into her belly. His hands traced her body, as if he was trying to memorize her form by touch alone. Shoulder. Arm. Waist. Thigh. Then his palm cupped her breast. His thumb brushed over her nipple, sending a rush of desire flowing across Madelyn's skin. He rolled her nipple between thumb and forefinger, pleasure and pain becoming one. She gasped and gripped his shoulders. His kisses moved from her lips to her neck, her shoulder, her breast. He took each nipple into his mouth in turn.

Right now, Madelyn's entire universe was in the cabin. She and Roman were the only two people in the world who mattered.

His mouth traveled lower, his tongue on her rib cage, her stomach. Lower still, until he knelt before her, worshipping at the altar of her sex. He explored her with his tongue, tasting and sucking. He slid one finger inside of her and then another. His fingers moved within her as his tongue and mouth took control.

Madelyn's veins filled with molten gold and from her core, a tide of pleasure began and spread outward. The swells grew until the tips of her fingers and the soles of her feet tingled. Then the waves rose, as Roman continued to attend to her with both mouth and hands, and she floated upon a great sea of bliss. Madelyn rode higher and higher and higher until she cried out with her climax. The echo of the receding surf resonated in her pulse and the salt spray mixed with the sweat that covered her skin.

Yet, she was far from being done.

Because after all this, now there was only one thing about which Madelyn was certain. She was going to make love to Roman DeMarco.

Her legs weak, Madelyn leaned into the wall at her back as Roman stood to face her. She kissed him, tasting the depth of her satisfaction, and worked the clasp free from his belt. Together, they wrestled his pants down just enough to free him. He reached around to his back pocket and pulled out his wallet and then the foil packet of a condom. He removed the translucent condom from the wrapper and she slid it over his length.

He kissed her again and gripped her thighs. Lifting her, Roman braced Madelyn against the wall and she wrapped her legs around his middle. He entered her in one stroke. Lips. Bodies. Sweat. Breath. Cries of pleasure filled the morning. Sunlight danced across their skin and cast their shadows on the floor. Their coupling was raw, primordial. As they moved together, each instinctively knowing the intricate steps of their dance. Only him. Only her.

Another orgasm clenched Madelyn. She held tighter to Roman's broad shoulders, her nails biting his skin—trying to find purchase. As her pulse slowed, Roman's hips rocked forward once, twice and once again. He threw his head back and moaned with pleasure.

They remained together, her legs around his middle, with him inside of her, for a minute longer before she slid from his grasp. His hands cupped her face as he gently placed his lips on hers. She savored the sweetness of the kiss, and at the same time wondered, *Now, how am I different?*

Propped up on his elbow, Roman lay on his side. Madelyn, having fallen into a comatose-like sleep after their lovemaking, lay next to him. They once again shared the sleeping bag. She had redressed in the sweatshirt and her panties. He wore his pants and nothing else. Her back was nestled into his chest. Her breaths were long and low. He needed to check on the generator, it should be fully charged soon, but he loathed the notion of leaving Madelyn's side.

The memory of being sheathed inside her came to him with excruciating clarity and he hardened. In her sleep, Madelyn stirred and arched her back—grinding into him more.

Roman felt his hips rock and fisted his hands as if in agony. He needed, wanted to make love to Madelyn again, and again, and again.

She yawned, and from his position over her shoulder, he saw her eyelashes flutter and open.

She was awake.

Roman could hardly be blamed for his physical reaction, and while he imagined she'd understand, he still felt like a creep of the first order. His heartbeat did a Sousa march.

"Well, that's a fine way to wake up," she said. Her voice was husky and slow.

"It's just that, well, I..."

"No need to explain," she said. She rolled over to face him. Her hand rubbed his crotch.

Roman sucked in a breath.

"I just want to know if you're prepared to use that weapon, Soldier?" she asked, teasing him in more ways than one.

He was, and then some. Roman's lips met hers, as Madelyn unfastened his pants and freed him. She circled his tip with a finger and collected a bead of moisture. Using his own lubrication, she slid her hand up and down his length. "I want you again, Roman," she said.

Up until now, Madelyn had been reluctant to become lovers, using biomedical mumbo jumbo as her excuse. And now she was ready for more?

Was Roman being used for sex? Was he annoyed by the idea? Definitely...maybe. He was realizing that he wanted more from Madelyn than simply a physical relationship—but they both had barriers to overcome. And yet, he could deny her nothing. That was true from the first moment he saw her and he saw that with startling clarity.

It was why he didn't make her leave The Prow

when she showed up at Oleg's office. It was why he came to cabin, where he knew she'd be safe, instead of going to Denver. It was why he agreed to find Ava when he had the world's greatest criminal to track down.

Her hand stopped moving and Roman could've wept.

"You don't have to quit," he said.

"I wasn't planning on it." Madelyn licked her open palm.

Roman hardened even further. She gripped him steadily, her strokes were long and slow. From the base to the tip and back again. He rolled to his back, giving her total access. But he wanted more from her.

"I need to be inside of you," he said, tugging Madelyn close to him. "Come here."

Pulling off her sweatshirt, Madelyn sat astride his waist. He slid into her with a single thrust. Moaning, she bent to him, kissed him. He cupped her breasts. They fit into his palms perfectly and her nipples hardened under his touch. Roman drove into Madelyn as she whimpered with pleasure. A shimmy ran through her body and Roman moved his hand to the top of her sex.

He stroked her, so hot and slick, that he almost lost control and climaxed himself. Sweat-slicked skin. Hot mouths. Eager tongues. Moans of ecstasy and cries of delight. Roman's senses were overloaded. It was more than the physicality of the moment, it was the fact that she made him whole.

Madelyn increased her pace, driving down on him harder. He matched her stroke for stroke as she glowed with perspiration.

She reared back and cried out. Her innermost muscles clenched as they came together. Only as the echo of his final throb faded did he think.

"Damn. No condom."

"It's okay," she said, "I'm on the pill and I've been tested for everything."

Roman had a full physical workup annually, and he'd practiced safe sex since his last doctor's visit. Still. "I should've taken care of you. I guess I got caught up in the moment." It was a lousy excuse.

"I did, too," she said as she snuggled into his chest.

Roman draped an arm over her shoulder and pulled her closer. She was soft and petite everywhere he was large and rough.

"But, I'm an adult, too, you know," she sighed. "I can take care of myself."

"I like taking care of you."

She kissed the inside of his wrist. "You know, if it weren't for you, I'd be dead now." She gave a little shiver. "So I'm glad I have someone watching out for me."

Her statement brought back the thought that had never left.

Roman had valuable information about Oleg Zavalov and, more important, Nikolai Mateev. Even though the obstacles before Roman were difficult, he could handle each step of the journey. The first step, the hardest one by far, would be to let go of Madelyn and return to the real world, especially since she wanted nothing more between them.

Oleg shifted in his seat. His eyes burned and his head throbbed. He tried to recall the last time he'd slept. Yesterday, he thought, or was it two days ago now? He refocused on the road as each revolution of the tires carried him closer. Closer to what, he didn't know. Either breathtaking glory or certain doom.

The phone in his pocket vibrated and chirped. He took his eyes from the road for a second to swipe to answer, then look at the caller.

A split second after he answered, he remembered: it wasn't even his phone.

Oleg's pulse spiked and he dropped his foot on the accelerator, as if he could outrun the person on the other line.

"Da," he answered. *Yes.*

"Serge?" Vomit rose in the back of Oleg's throat. He'd only spoken to Nikolai Mateev twice before, but he'd recognize the gravelly and deep voice anywhere.

"Net, eto Oleg." *No, this is Oleg.*

"Oleg? Why do you have Serge's phone?"

The memory of Serge, laid out on the floor of the beer cooler, returned to Oleg. He had tried to be careful by shutting down the bar right after finding the body, but Nikolai had eyes and ears everywhere. What had he heard? What did Nikolai suspect?

"He's busy," Oleg said, giving the first lie that came to mind.

"Well, then, I will speak to you. I need to be picked up at eight o'clock. You will be ready. My nephew will be ready. My money will be ready."

Nikolai's money—two million dollars in US currency—was in a dozen different accounts throughout the state. It would take Oleg hours, no days, to liquidate it all. Per the GPS, he had another hour to the road—perhaps too long of a trip for a hunch. Maybe he'd be better served by turning around and dealing with the cash.

"Everything will be as you want," he said to Nikolai. Oleg had no idea how to keep his promise, yet there was nothing else for him to say. He waited a beat for Nikolai's response. Then a moment more. He pulled the phone from his ear and stared at the screen.

It was blank. Nikolai had hung up.

Oleg examined the phone and withdrew his own cell from his pocket. Then Anton's, as well. They were all the exact same. It should have been an inconsequential detail. Instead, it had been an important fact, and one that Oleg was foolish to have missed.

"Chert." Damn.

Returning his own phone to his pocket, Oleg threw the other phones to the passenger seat. Had Nikolai believed him, or was Oleg being set up?

Roman knelt before the fire and stoked the flames. He peered at the ravioli that had been set over the fire to cook. Steam rose from the pot and the sauce began to bubble.

"Can you watch this?" he asked Madelyn. "The generator's charged enough to use the radio now. Once I've broadcast on RMJ's secure channel, we'll eat and then leave. It'll give the crew in Denver enough time to meet us at the creek."

Madelyn rose from the sleeping bag. After wiggling into her jeans, she slipped back on the sweatshirt. It was a crime to cover up such beauty, but Roman said nothing.

She traded places with him at the hearth and scraped the sides of the pot. "How will we cross the creek when we get there. The volume of water was strong."

"The folks from RMJ will bring a rope to throw across the stream and a life preserver. It's what I'd do."

"They're professionals, right?" she said, dishing out the pasta.

"We all are." Roman accepted the bowl and spoon, liking the fact they were sharing another meal a little too much, and turned to the generator. He took a big bite, the roof of his mouth burning, but he didn't care about the discomfort. "Damn it," he cursed. "Damn it, damn it, damn it."

"It is hot," Madelyn said. "I should've warned you."

"Not the ravioli." He didn't care about food anymore. "The generator." He slapped the top, the side, the top. "It was fifty percent charged just a minute ago, and now there's nothing. Something is wrong."

"Which means what? You have more work to do?"

Roman looked out the window. The sun was almost at its zenith, and half the daylight was gone. He could stay and work on both the generator and the radio, hoping that next time he actually fixed them both.

And if he didn't?

He couldn't waste any more time. Roman had to act. He scooped several bites of ravioli into his mouth, chewed quickly and swallowed. "If I leave now, I can make it to the road in an hour—maybe two."

"But what about the creek? You said it was treacherous."

"I'll be fine."

"Or you might not. Last night you had hypothermia. Dousing yourself in cold water is never a good idea. In this instance, it might be deadly."

"The sun's out, it's getting warmer."

"Which means more runoff from the snowmelt, which means faster running and colder water. It's a bad idea for you to be out there alone."

How long had it been since someone cared for Roman's well-being? How long had it been since it mattered if they did? Then again, maybe she was only concerned about him in a medical sense, not a personal one. Their dual session of passion notwithstanding, she'd made it clear that she didn't want any romantic entanglements.

He turned his mind from all things emotional and focused on a more comfortable subject: work. Roman had one hell of an important job—cold water be damned. "This is the plan. I'm leaving now. You stay here. I can make seven miles in an hour and may even get lucky and find someone on the road who'll give me a lift. Once I contact my team and let them know that Mateev is on his way to Boulder, I'll send someone up to get you. You have food, shelter, water, heat to last you several days, but someone will get you by tomorrow morning, at the latest."

"Oh no, no, no." Madelyn shook her head. "You aren't leaving me."

Roman paused, the constriction of indecision—like a shirt, two sizes too small—left him uncomfortable. Without question, Madelyn would be safer if she remained. He would be faster alone, too. At the same time, he wanted her with him. Besides, they worked well together as a team and she had skills—medically speaking—that he didn't.

She said, "I'm not going to argue and I'm not going to take no for an answer."

He believed her on both counts.

Once again on the same hill, Madelyn walked in silence next to Roman, consumed by her thoughts. She couldn't believe that she'd had sex with a man she barely knew. But in many ways, she knew him better than she would have if they'd been together for years.

What they lacked was a history together. Did that mean that she shouldn't care?

There was another problem, as well. While she technically had a prescription for birth control pills, Madelyn had not taken one in more than forty-eight hours. She'd missed one night because of rounds at the hospital and another because, well, her life had been shaken and stirred when she'd met Roman for the first time. And she was midcycle, prime time for fertility. She toyed with the idea of saying something to Roman. After all, there had been two of them in that sleeping bag. But to what end? Especially since the possibility of a pregnancy was still statistically low.

"What will happen once we get back to Boulder?" she asked, the silence and her thoughts too much.

Roman shook his head. He carried a backpack filled with food, water, the flashlight and a utility knife. "We have to head straight to Denver and my office."

"Shouldn't we talk to the police first? You know, make a statement?"

"RMJ will get in touch with the FBI on our behalf."

They walked side by side. Their hands close, but not touching. Madelyn thought of winding her fingers through his. They'd made love twice and it seemed natural to continue the connection. She moved to him, their fingers grazing, an electric surge traveling up her arm. But she stepped away. Hadn't she warned of artificial feelings postcoitus? Funny enough, though, her affections for Roman felt true.

"You're an amazing woman, Madelyn Thompkins," Roman said. "Maybe when all this is over, we can get together."

"And do what?" she asked, being purposefully obtuse.

"I don't know," said Roman, "We can have dinner that doesn't come out of a can."

Her pulse raced with the possibility. Yet, the razor's edge she had to walk every day didn't allow for foolish love affairs that left her breathless and her mind wandering. One misstep and she could lose her place in med school. Once she was a doctor, it wouldn't get any better. Medical mistakes ended lives. "I'm busy," she said.

"I didn't ask you about a specific day or time yet."

"It doesn't matter," she said. "I'm busy all the time."

"I understand," he said, his tone steely. "Like I said, no pressure from me."

I understand. Madelyn doubted very much that Roman did.

Even if she cared for Roman it didn't change how much time and energy she devoted to her studies, or that he would eventually tire of her focus being on something other than him. Then there was a part of her that wanted Roman to press and cajole her into going out on a date. But he hadn't.

Roman, unaware of her mental struggle, spoke up. "In terms of your schedule, until Oleg Zavalov has been arrested, you might need to be placed in protective custody. The FBI will take you to a secure sight, probably a hotel in another area, where agents will be with you around the clock."

"Protective custody? No way. I have classes and my work at the hospital. I can't hide out in some sketchy motel room in another part of the state."

"I'd actually prefer that they took you halfway across the country, but let's wait to see what arrangements can be made. Maybe you can have a police detail stay with you 24/7."

"My patients won't be happy. Neither will the hospital, or my professors."

"Would they rather attend your funeral?"

Madelyn's jaw tightened. He had a point.

The sun continued to climb in the sky, promising a warm, bright and clear day—the kind for which Colorado was famous.

They came upon Madelyn's car, left at an angle on the rutted dirt road. She stroked it from fender to bumper, as if it were an ailing pet.

"Does this road go anywhere beyond the safe house?" Madelyn asked.

"No," said Roman, "all of this land is private. So, if you're worried about someone trying to get past you or stealing your car—don't."

She nodded as if he'd cleared up every concern, but there was still the question of getting her car back to Boulder and in working order again. How much would the repair bill be, along with a tow back to town? A semester's worth of expenses? More?

Madelyn gave the hood a final pat. Then again, she had begun this journey to find her sister, and there was no car on the earth that was worth more than Ava's life.

They trekked on. The sun continued to climb and warm the thin mountain air. Sweat damped Madelyn's back and chest. The creek, a brown serpent, came into view. She removed her blazer, tied it around her waist and moved to the bank. Murky water rushed past, foaming at points where broken branches tangled together and slowed the flow. Madelyn sucked in a breath. "That's a lot of water," she said.

"I can't wait another day. Hell, I can't wait another hour to get in contact with RMJ," Roman said as he massaged the back of his neck. "Which means I have to get to the other side of this stream, and this is the narrowest span for miles. I wish we had another option."

"I'm going to loop one arm through my backpack's strap and you hold on to the other one. If you fall into the water and we get separated, flip on your back and put your feet downstream. Don't try to stand up or swim against the current."

"Feet downstream," she repeated. "Don't swim against the current and don't try to stand up."

"The most important thing to remember is to not panic. Panicking gets you hurt."

She wound her arm through the backpack strap and mentally repeated the instructions as they stepped off the bank. Within seconds, Madelyn had frigid water swirling around her knees. The current, a hand of ice, tried to push her over with unrelenting determination.

Underfoot, the creek bed was uneven, rocky and slick with silt. She stubbed her toe, slid and wavered. She held out her arms for balance and the backpack fell from her arm.

Roman gripped her elbow. "Steady," he said. "Slow and steady."

Madelyn tried to speak, but could not find her voice. She nodded and gripped the strap. Her fingers were thick and at the same time brittle—like the dried limbs of a long-dead tree.

"Eight feet gone, ten feet to go," said Roman. "We're almost halfway there."

Madelyn knew he was lying. The creek was more than two dozen feet across, which left them less than a third of the way done. Even though she was only submerged to the knee, cold crept out of the water and traveled upward into her thighs, pelvis and torso. She wasn't sure she could make it to the opposite bank. Yet, she had to ask herself—did she have another choice?

One step, she said to herself. One step closer to the bank. One step closer to getting out of the freezing water. One step closer to finding Ava, and getting her help.

One more step...

The ground beneath Madelyn's feet disappeared and the sky overhead went black. Murky darkness surrounded her. She was freezing. It was a bitter and biting cold she'd never felt before. Struggling, fighting her way to the surface, Madelyn cried for help. Her mouth filled with water and she coughed, her lungs filling even as she expelled the dirty liquid. Reaching again for the surface, she found only rocks and sand. Madelyn thrashed, searching for purchase and seeking air, but the stream kept her down, pulling her along to a dark, cold place...

Chapter 7

Roman stepped into a hole, a deep divide in the middle of the stream. Cold water punched him in the gut, stealing his breath and pinching his chest in a vise. The backpack looped through his arm lightened and floated on top of the water. He turned for Madelyn.

She was gone.

He drew a deep breath and dove beneath the surface. The muddy water stung his eyes, the silt so thick that it rendered him blind. He reached out, waving his arms, hoping to connect with flesh or cloth or hair. Anything. There was nothing. His lungs burned and he surfaced. She was still gone, vanished, but she was close—he refused to believe anything less.

Another breath. Another trip into the icy, dark abyss.

Roman pushed off from the bottom, letting the current carry him downstream. He waved his arms before him in a wide arc. He kicked out, propelling himself forward and sweeping his arms back and forth the whole time. Again, his breath gave out and he surfaced, gasping.

How long had Madelyn been under? Soon, he wouldn't be searching for Madelyn, but rather her corpse. Roman would be damned if he was going to let that happen.

He took another breath, filling his lungs past the point of pain. The current pressed him down and dragged him along the bottom. His knees connected with something solid. He felt pressure, but not the blinding flash of pain he would expect from bone striking against a rock. Whatever he'd hit was soft and malleable. He pictured a lifeless hand floating in the current.

Roman twisted around, and his fingers danced along the streambed. His lungs burned. His legs and feet cramped painfully and every cell in his body screamed for life-giving oxygen. He refused to give up. He turned again and searched the stream bottom again, inch by slow inch.

It had been her. He knew it. And if he surfaced now, she would be lost. Then again, if he didn't get some air and out of the cold water, he'd be lost, as well.

One more foot. Just one more.

His fingers were well past numb but they brushed against something fluid, like the creek but with substance. It was fabric. His fist closed.

Keeping his grip firm, Roman pulled himself toward the cloth. It was Madelyn. He quickly found one shoulder and then the other. Arms hooked underneath, he pushed up and broke the surface. Madelyn's head lolled to the side, her skin was pale and her lips were blue. He felt for a pulse and found none.

"Madelyn?" He shook her and slapped each cheek. "Madelyn?"

The current buffeted against Roman, setting him off balance and pulling Madelyn in a deadly game of tug-of-war.

"I have to get you to land," he said. He refused to believe that she couldn't hear him, that she would never hear him again. "We'll get you dry and warm." He'd found a place where he could stand again in the middle of the stream as he considered his next steps.

Head back to his cabin? Or continue to the opposite bank? He'd been in the water before and knew it was much shallower closer to the other side. While the cabin offered shelter, food and warmth, he didn't know if he had the strength to fight the deepest part of the creek again.

Better to get out of the water and worry about the rest later. Cradling Madelyn's head in the crook of his arm, he moved to the opposite bank. The water level dropped, leaving Roman submerged only to his shins. He hefted Madelyn onto his shoulder and ran the rest of the way. He scrambled up a wall of mud and laid her on the dusty road.

Once again, he felt for a pulse, hopeful that he'd missed it the first time. It wasn't there. He listened for breath. Nothing; not that he had expected any better. Roman had used lifesaving measures before. Each incident brought him to a different gate of hell as he fought for the life of a friend or a brother in arms. But this time was different. Madelyn was his lover, and her caress still lingered on his skin. Her kiss remained on his lips.

Placing one hand atop the other, Roman pressed down on Madelyn's chest. Once. Twice. Three times. Four times. He tilted her head back, pinched her nose and exhaled into her mouth. Her chest rose as it filled with air. Yet, the breath was artificial and she took none on her own.

Compress. Compress. Compress. Compress. Breathe.

He refused to consider that she might be gone— dead and gone—yet he could think of nothing else.

Compress. Compress. Compress. Compress. Breathe.

He already knew, deep down, that the only thing worth caring about was her safety. Or that he would risk his own operation—heck, his own life—for her.

Suddenly, Madelyn's chest heaved. She bucked and coughed. He gently rolled her to her side, lest she choke. She wheezed and spat muddy water onto the dirt road.

She pulled her knees to her chest and began to tremble.

Roman lifted her head into his lap and stroked a tuft of hair off her forehead.

"I," she croaked, as her eyes found his. "What happened?"

"Nothing happened," said Roman. His head buzzed and his chest filled with warmth. He wiped at a leaky eye with his knuckle. "I promised to keep you safe and I did."

"Did I drown?"

She stared up at him with her big, brown eyes. Her hair was slicked back and her lips still held a hint of purple. She was beautiful, fragile as the single petal on a rose and yet stronger than granite. He tried to tell her that when he pulled her from the water she was dead. The truth lay heavy on his tongue and held the taste of panic—iron mixed with salt. "There was a hole in the middle of the stream. You slipped and went under."

"Then you saved my life, again."

"Don't say it like that, you make me sound like a superhero or something. I look bad in a cape, worse in tights."

She smiled. "You are a hero, though. To me, anyway."

Before he could think of a reply, a cloud of dust caught his eye. Roman stood and shielded his eyes with a hand. A black sedan, turned dull and gray with a coating of dust, sped up the road. A car? Here?

"It looks like we have unexpected company," he said. "This is a private road, so uninvited guests are never good."

"Or maybe it's someone from your agency. They could have started searching for you and by now, figured you might be here."

"That's possible," Roman said, sounding dubious.

He helped Madelyn to her feet. Still weak from her time in the water, she leaned into him. Until they knew who was in the car, they should run—or at least hide. Yet, she didn't have the energy to move far. He could carry her, but could he move fast enough for them to hide? Then again, how much time would he lose if they got lost in the woods?

That meant only one thing, Roman had to stand his ground and face whoever was coming.

A cloud of dust surrounded Oleg's car, obscuring the road and convincing him that coming out here was a fool's errand. And Oleg was never a fool. He turned on the windshield wipers, a half-moon of clean appeared. Leaning forward in his seat, he looked for a spot wide enough to turn around.

Then he saw them. Two figures standing in the middle of the road. Even from a distance, Oleg recognized Madelyn and Roman. Through the grimy windshield, he assessed their state—the matted hair, the soaking clothes—and could tell they were drenched. Madelyn clung to Roman's arm. Despite the sun, she shivered. The creek behind them ran black and thick with rushing water. Supports from a bridge that was no longer there stood as a warning to any who might try and cross. But they had dared, Oleg would bet his life.

If Oleg believed in a higher power, he would have offered up a prayer of thanks. But, he didn't. As far as he was concerned, mankind had been flung upon the earth and left to make their own way.

As he pulled up, turning the car so it blocked the road, he congratulated himself for his intelligence and daring. The two soaking wet people in the road were obviously Oleg's reward for being superior to his opposition.

From the glove box, he withdrew a gun. Then he opened the door and got out of the car, saying nothing. The silence he felt was more foreboding than any warning or taunt he might deliver. He aimed and pulled the trigger.

The crack of the bullet shot through the air. The report thundered, echoing off the mountains before fading into nothing. Grit and dust billowed into the air. When the cloud cleared, Roman was on the ground. He lay atop Madelyn, shielding her with his body. Both were still unfortunately alive and uninjured, although they were both pinned down and in the open.

Oleg lined up the sights between Roman's shoulders. A hit to the spine and Roman Black would be no more. He only needed one person to account to Nikolai for Serge's death, and Oleg knew that controlling Madelyn would be easier than restraining Roman. She was weak where Roman was strong.

Oleg steadied his arm and wrapped his finger around the trigger, inhaling deeply as he prepared to pull again...

The scene changed in an instant. A dark shape rushed toward Oleg and before he could react, the car door slammed into him. Breath was forced from his lungs and the gun skittered from his grasp. Roman grabbed Oleg by the lapel and shoved his knee in Oleg's middle. Vomit erupted from Oleg in a hot spew that ran down his shirt.

A punch to the face and Oleg's ears buzzed, his vision darkening at the edges. An elbow was dropped on the crook of his shoulder, the exact place where it became his neck and world tilted. Oleg staggered before sprawling on the ground.

Roman hoisted him to his feet. "How'd you find us? Who told you about this place?"

Oleg managed a smile. "Wouldn't you love to know."

"I've been waiting a long time to take you in," Roman said as he dragged Oleg to the back of the car.

Well, this wasn't a good situation. At. All.

With Oleg in custody, Nikolai Mateev would never find the money that Oleg had laundered and then hidden away. Even in his beaten and beleaguered state, Oleg knew that two million US dollars was not a sum to overlook. So, if Oleg went to prison, he would be punished twice. Once by the justice system, with a lengthy sentence and relinquishment of his assets. Then again, by Nikolai as he exacted two million dollars' worth of revenge.

Because even in prison, Nikolai Mateev would be able to find him. And his punishment would be painful.

Fueled by desperation, strength surged through him. He pulled away and he tumbled to the ground.

Clawing forward, he scrambled to his feet.

"Stop! Or I'll shoot." Oleg turned to the voice. Madelyn Thompkins held his gun.

"You plan to shoot?" he asked. His lips were inflamed, and each word tasted of agony. "Go ahead." He spat blood on the ground. "Shoot."

Who would have thought he could feel such hatred for this woman?

Legs braced against the ground, Madelyn kept the barrel trained on him. She didn't fire. He didn't think she would. But it brought up another interesting dynamic. Whoever held the gun had all the power. And power was exactly what Oleg needed.

"Madelyn," Roman said, "give me the gun."

Oleg shuffled forward, remaining between Madelyn and Roman, his gaze locked with hers. He lurched toward her, reaching for the gun. Light flashed from the muzzle.

Oleg fell forward. Liquid hands of ice pulled him into the darkness. His lungs filled with water. *I've been shot*, he thought, stunned, and then...blackness.

Madelyn stumbled back, her arm springing upward with the gun's recoil. Oleg had disappeared, but it hadn't been magic—she'd shot him. Her arm trembled. She felt like throwing up. The gun slipped from her fingers onto the ground as she dived toward the creek.

She had to save him. She was sworn to protect life, not take it. Madelyn slipped off her shoes and untied the jacket from her waist.

"You aren't going anywhere." Roman held her back, his large hand on her shoulder. He moved Oleg's gun to the waistband of his pants.

His touch was strong and warm. She wanted to turn all her burdens over to him. "I can't just let him die."

"You almost drowned while we were crossing that stream, Madelyn." Roman pulled her into an embrace. "I'm not letting you kill yourself trying to save Oleg Zavalov."

She pushed against him and he held her tighter.

"I'll walk alongside the creek and try to find him." Roman steered her toward the car. "You wait here."

"I can walk with you."

"It's just that…"

Madelyn had never seen Roman at a loss for words. His silence crept across her skin, lifting gooseflesh in its wake. She shivered. "It's just that, what?"

"You shot him."

"I did." The words were heavy on her tongue. "That's why I need to find him."

He looked upstream, then back at her. "I'd really rather you stay here."

Why was Roman being so elusive? "Are you worried that I might have killed Oleg and you don't want me to see his body?"

He exhaled and nodded. "Something like that. It's hard to take a life. Even a justified killing is difficult."

Justified killing. She clenched her teeth against the phrase, as if it were medicine that someone was forcing her to swallow. Madelyn imagined the firearm in her hand. The heft, the recoil, the bite. She saw Oleg's swollen eyes, suddenly wide, as he was whirled around, and then his back as he toppled from view.

Oleg Zavalov was unquestionably a vile man, but he was still a man. Didn't the propensity for both good and evil reside in every human heart? Oleg must have loved someone. Someone must have loved him in return. And now all that was left were empty memories of those affections.

She sank to her knees. Gravel bit into her flesh, each imprint a painful reminder of what she had done when terror had taken over and she'd pulled the trigger. Roman placed his hand on her shoulder. She gripped his fingers with her own.

"You were very brave," he said.

"I shot an unarmed man. That makes me a coward," she said, her words came out with a sob. "I was afraid to shoot him. But more afraid of what would happen if I didn't."

"Remember what I said about bravery?" Roman asked.

"Not really," she said, "but, I'm not in the mood to be lectured."

"Bravery," he began, ignoring her words completely, "isn't the lack of fear, but the ability to act even though you are afraid."

"It's a nice sentiment," she said. The pain in her head lessened.

"It's true," said Roman. He held out his hand to her and Madelyn let him help her to her feet. "I'll see if Oleg washed up downstream," he said.

"I'm going with you." Madelyn stepped back into her shoes and retied the blazer around her waist. "Whatever the outcome, I need to know."

Roman just nodded and led the way as they picked along the creek's edge. Trees and bushes grew right up to the bank, making their search difficult. After a half a mile of walking, Roman stopped. "See that," he said. An eddy swirled, filled with twigs and leaves. Amid the debris was a man's shoe—a black loafer, and leather from the looks of it.

Roman broke a dead branch from a tree and fished the shoe from the water. "High-end Italian," he said as he read the inside label. "It's Oleg's. I've seen him wear this shoe hundreds of times."

"Then where is he?"

"There's no telling. He might be close or miles away. What I do know is that right now we are wasting our time by looking."

"You can't say that."

Roman pulled her close. She allowed herself to be

enveloped in his embrace. "Let's get back to the car. At least we have a way back to town. Once we can make a call, we'll have search and rescue out here looking for him. They're the professionals. We aren't."

Again, he made sense. Madelyn nodded, happy that he'd decided, and for once she wasn't left to make important decisions on her own. She was happier still that this nightmare might finally be ending.

They fought their way back through the scrub to the road. In their haste to leave, they hadn't bothered to turn off Oleg's car or shut the door. The ding, ding, ding of a warning bell overrode the rushing water and the call of the birds. A cloud of exhaust billowed around the car, a dirty fog hovering above it all.

Roman opened the passenger door and she slipped into the leather seat. She was beyond fatigued and felt as if she could sleep for a year. Despite all the dangers of the past day and a half, in many ways the time had been special for Madelyn, magical almost. But as they drove away from the creek, she understood that the spell between her and Roman was ending.

If they were lucky, then soon their lives would return to normal. And those normal lives did not include each other. Not long ago, she'd made a grand pronouncement that any feelings of affection were simply an alluring cocktail of brain chemicals and echoes from a prehistoric need to reproduce. If that was all that she was experiencing, then why was Madelyn's chest hollow, aching with a need for Roman to somehow complete her?

The feeling gave her pause. As the car bounced and jostled over the dirt track, Madelyn wondered, how could she think of needing someone to complete her? All along, she had seen a serious relationship as a pitfall to be avoided.

She leaned into the seat and closed her eyes. Her very busy, but clear-cut life had spiraled out of control. So much in fact, that she no longer controlled her own emotions. Roman pulled hard on the steering wheel. The car turned right and slammed onto the paved road. From beneath her seat two cell phones slid forward and clattered against her ankles.

"Look what we have here." Madelyn held up the two identical phones.

Roman pulled to the shoulder and took the phones from her hand.

He tried to open both before saying, "Passcode protected. I could break through, but I have a better idea. If Oleg has programmed either number into his car, then I should be able to call one of them. Once we answer, we're in."

"If this car has its own phone system, why not call out directly with that?" Madelyn asked.

"It'll only work if one of these belongs to Oleg. Otherwise we can only use his contact list." Roman hit the button for the car's phone system.

"Call Oleg," he said. Both phones remained silent. He ended the connection and tried again. "Call Serge."

A phone lit up and trilled. Roman swiped and answered, then ended the call again. He made another call that was answered by three beeps. After he entered a four-digit passcode and disconnected, it rang again.

"Roman." She recognized the voice at once. It was Roman's boss, the Brit. "Where are you? I got a message last night and then you fell of the map."

Roman exhaled, the tension in his shoulders slipped away. "It's good to hear your voice, Ian," he said, relieved to have finally made contact. He eased back on to the road. For the next ten minutes, Roman drove and filled Ian in on the developments of the case—their wild night at The Prow, Madelyn and her search for Ava, Oleg and his cronies, and Nikolai Mateev.

He told Ian about his theory that Oleg had discovered Madelyn's identity, and how he somehow found the safe house. Roman ended with Oleg being shot, although he didn't mention that it was Madelyn who had pulled the trigger.

"Oleg's body is missing," he concluded, "but we did find his shoe."

For a long moment, the call was silent. Roman wondered if they'd lost contact on the mountainous road.

"Are you still there?" Roman asked, as the pause stretched out.

Ian came onto the line. "Are you sure," he said, his words slow and precise, "that Nikolai Mateev is coming to Boulder?"

"I'm positive that's what Oleg said. He's expected today, if what I heard was right."

"Any idea how? Auto? Air?"

"I didn't get a travel itinerary, brother. Sorry."

"The first thing we need to do is to get you and Miss Thompkins back to Denver." A constant clicking served as a background to Ian's words. Roman envisioned his boss and friend sitting behind his desk—a big wooden thing with scrollwork on the front panel and a leather ink blotter on top. The speakerphone was at his elbow, while his fingers danced over the keyboard of his desktop computer. "There's a truck stop forty miles south of where you are. It's busy, which is good and bad. Bad because you'll be seen, and there's no telling by whom. Good because you'll likely blend in, just two more travelers out of many. Park there and I'll pick you up personally."

"I'm not sure that leaving the car is our best play. I can easily drive directly to the office and not waste more time."

"In one of your previous reports you said there were two Russian nationalists working for Oleg."

"Anton and Serge," Roman said. "And we don't know what Oleg told Anton or where he is now." He was itching to get back to Denver, but understood that in his haste he could lead Anton to the RMJ offices and compromise the case even more. "I guess it really is better to be safe than sorry."

"Park the car where it won't look abandoned,"

said Ian. Roman didn't need the added direction. After all, he'd been with Delta Force for years and knew all about covert operations. "I'll meet you in forty-five minutes."

Roman ended the call.

"What now?" Madelyn asked.

He glanced at her. Dark circles ringed her eyes, making her milky complexion paler. Her lips were still tinged with purple, like she'd been eating blackberries. Blackberries and cream, now that was a delicious combination. Like her.

He shook off the errant sexy thought and focused on the situation. "You should rest," he said. He turned on the seat warmer and looked back at the road. "It's out of our hands now. All we can do is cross our fingers and hope that the good guys win."

Madelyn napped while Roman drove. He kept the radio off, the softly purring engine more musical than any song. The truck stop came into view and he eased into a space halfway down a row filled with a variety of cars. Madelyn roused as he turned off the engine.

Stretching, she glanced out the window. "That was the fastest forty minutes of my life," she joked.

He'd come to appreciate her corny quips and would miss them once the case ended. Too bad he couldn't convince her to give the two of them a chance— maybe something could work out. But he got it, at one time—Roman had serious life goals, too.

On the other hand, just because she wouldn't go

out with him didn't mean that he cared any less. He hoped that she could retain her sense of humor. Soon Oleg's body would wash up, and though she'd never be charged with a crime—the shooting had been un-questionably self-defense—she'd have to live with the fact that she'd taken a life. No matter the reason, killing a person was never a laughing matter.

"Our job is to blend," he said. "Let's go inside. It'll arouse less suspicion than if we just sit in the car."

He pocketed the keys and both cell phones before opening his door and rounding to the other side of the car to help Madelyn out. He scanned the faces of everyone they passed, searching for one he rec-ognized. He saw no one. Leading Madelyn through the front doors, he made his way to a diner that took up half the truck stop and chose a booth in the back corner.

The scent of cooking beef, along with the smell of thick and meaty gravy, hung in the air. His mouth watered and his stomach rumbled. Too bad they wouldn't have time to grab a quick lunch. Half of a can of pasta was not enough food for a big guy like Roman. A waitress in a white uniform approached the table, order pad and pen in hand. "Can I get you something to drink while you look over the menu?" she asked.

"We won't be eating," Roman said. "But you can bring me a soda."

The waitress turned to Madelyn. "And you?"

"Nothing, thank you."

"You need something," Roman said. "You've had quite a morning and need to keep your strength up."

"No, thank you." Madelyn's teeth were clenched.

"Just bring her a soda, too," Roman said to the waitress. "If she doesn't drink it, I will."

"I'm not hungry," Madelyn said, once the waitress had left with their order. "Or thirsty. In fact, I feel queasy."

It was a physical sign of shock or even post-traumatic stress but Roman said nothing. "Just humor me and take the drink. Like I said, we need to blend in. If Anton comes here and asks questions, we don't want the waitress to remember the woman who sat in a restaurant and didn't order anything."

"Sorry," she said. "I hadn't thought of it that way..."

Her words were cut short by the waitress's return. She set their drinks on the table along with two straws wrapped in paper. "I'll stop back in a minute to see if you need refills," she said.

Roman thanked her and cast his gaze around the restaurant, the attached convenience store and the parking lot beyond. Even from his strategic location, it was hard to see everything. There were four security cameras on the premises, though. One behind the cash register, one at the door and one each trained on the two banks of fuel pumps. So far, Roman and Madelyn had avoided them all.

And since they had a few minutes to spare and a certain amount of privacy provided by the booth, he withdrew the cell phones from his pocket and laid them both on the table.

"They look identical," Madelyn noted.

"They are." He lifted one. "This is Serge's, so we have to assume that Oleg found his body in the beer cooler. It doesn't clear up the mystery of how he found us, though."

Madelyn lifted both shoulders and let them drop with a sigh. "I have no idea."

Neither did he, but it was a breach of RMJ's security and would warrant further investigation. "And this phone." He picked up the other one and gave it a little shake. "I have no idea whose phone this is."

"Can you open either? Maybe there's something useful in the emails or texts."

Roman bypassed the password on Serge's phone and then opened the web browser and found nothing of interest. The emails, texts and voice mail all had their own password protection. Aha. Too bad Roman never bet, because odds were that important communications went back and forth through those applications. "I can open everything eventually," he said, closing Serge's phone again. "But not now. I need equipment and more time. And speaking of time, Ian should be here any minute."

Roman lifted the cup to his lips, using it as cover while he glanced at the parking lot. The sun glinted off the windshield of a forest green luxury SUV as it drove in front of the travel plaza. Roman fished a slightly damp ten-dollar bill from his wallet, plenty for the drinks and a generous tip, and threw it on the table.

"That's our ride," he said, scooping up both phones and placing them in his pocket.

He kept his head down and positioned himself between Madelyn and the camera at the exit. The car pulled into a space well away from the building and Roman led Madelyn across the parking lot at a brisk walk. He opened the back door for Madelyn. After sliding in beside her, Roman pulled the door closed.

Ian sat in the driver's seat. As always, he was dressed in a suit, shirt and tie. His dark blond hair was short and swept off his face. His grey eyes were rimmed with red.

"Good to see you, Ian."

"It's good to be seen by you."

"Madelyn, let me introduce you to my boss, Sir Ian Wallace. Ian, this is Madelyn Thompkins."

Ian flashed a rare smile. "It's a pleasure to meet you."

The apples on Madelyn's cheeks reddened and she returned the smile, but reached for Roman's hand. Roman felt a pulling in his chest at her touch.

"You didn't have to come out and get me personally, Ian," Roman said, dragging his attention away from his feelings for Madelyn and returning them to the case. "I'm sure there's a lot that needs to be done."

"All that could wait. Besides, I wasn't going to let someone else have the pleasure of saving your butt."

"I saved my own butt, thank you very much."

Then to Madelyn he explained, "Ian is one of those friends who can always be counted on to help, and to be a smart-ass in the process."

Madelyn laughed. Being able to hear her giggle raised his spirits.

"And speaking of things that need done." Roman withdrew the two cell phones from a pocket on his thigh. He leaned forward, the seat belt tight across his chest. "This phone belonged to Serge. I used it to call you. The voice mail, texts and phone have a separate passcode, but can easily be circumvented once I get back to the office. This phone—" he held up the spare "—is a mystery. It's not Oleg's but was found in his car." More pockets still. "And here are the keys to Oleg's car. I parked in the fifth row back, center of the aisle."

"It looks like you've continued to be busy."

"It's what you pay me for."

"Madelyn?" Ian began. "Did Roman tell you that he was the very first person I brought on to the RMJ team?"

"Actually," she said, "he did."

"Really? Anything else interesting he shared with you?"

"He said that the first time you two met that you called him a bloke."

Ian used the rearview mirror and made eye contact with Roman. "Is she teasing me?"

"She likes jokes, brother."

"Then she's perfect for you." Ian paused. "*Bloke.*

In all honesty, I'm glad to see that you're both in good spirits. And since you're here now, let's talk business. I've contacted all the players from the task force. FBI. DEA. Colorado Bureau of Investigation. They've been notified that our main target, Nikolai Mateev, is en route."

"Nikolai Mateev?" Madelyn asked. "The Russian mobster?"

Ian looked at Roman through the rearview mirror again. This time, he lifted a single brow. Roman ignored the stare and the question that was certain to go along with it—*What exactly have you told this woman?*

"And what about my sister, Ava?" Madelyn asked. "Roman mentioned to you that she's been out of contact for months. I saw her social media post from The Prow last night. It's what drew me into this mess."

"She hasn't been located. In truth, we haven't launched an all-out search," Ian said. "The Boulder PD are looking, though."

Madelyn flopped into her seat. Hand in chin, she looked out the window. "It feels like I should be able to do more."

"Because of you," said Roman, "we have information about one of the biggest drug dealers in the world. Not just Boulder, or Colorado, or even the United States. Putting Nikolai Mateev in jail will make life better for a lot of people."

"My sister included?"

"A lot of that depends on Ava and her choices."

Madelyn fell silent.

The SUV rolled on, making its way to the nearby interstate and soon they were traveling southward to Denver. Their passage slowed only a little as they encountered traffic in the metro area and before Roman knew it, Ian was pulling into the parking garage connected to Rocky Mountain Justice's Sixteenth Street Mall office building.

As soon as the car stopped, Roman opened the door and helped Madelyn from the Range Rover. Their palms met. Her skin was soft and warm.

"Roman!" Katarina, the resident communications expert ran out and met the SUV as it parked. In her late forties, Kat lived the outdoor lifestyle of cycling, skiing and whitewater kayaking and was as fit as the rest of the operatives.

Grabbing Roman by the shoulder, she whirled him around, before folding him into her strong arms. "I'm so glad that you're safe," she said.

"It's good to be back," Roman said.

His gaze found Madelyn. Ian had taken her by the elbow and led her away, all the while giving the history of RMJ. Roman had heard it all before—beginning with a speech about Ian's crusade for a world free of injustice. Ian opened the fire door that separated the parking garage from the office suite and ushered Madelyn inside, talking all the while. The door slammed shut and she was gone.

A hot bubble of jealousy rose within Roman and his jaw tightened. Then the bubble burst and disappeared. Ian was Roman's boss and best friend. Never would he betray their bond.

As they made their way through the cavernous parking garage, Kat reached for the door handle and paused. "So, who is she?"

"Madelyn Thompkins," Roman said. "Med student at CU. She came to The Prow looking for her sister who's been AWOL since a stint at rehab. Collateral damage to the extreme, just in the wrong place at the wrong time."

"Who is she to you?"

"Is it that obvious?"

"Sure is," said Katarina. "You held the door open for her."

"A guy can't be a gentleman nowadays? What's the world coming to?"

"And you sat in the back with her, not up front with Ian—even though you are his right-hand man."

"I thought *you* were his right-hand man."

"Now who's not being a gentleman," she teased in return. "Besides, I could tell that she's more than collateral damage the minute I saw the way you looked at her."

"Yeah?" Roman asked. "How's that?"

Katarina pulled the metal door open. As Roman stepped through, she said, "You looked at her, my friend, like you've fallen hard."

The break room in the RMJ offices was unremarkable. An obligatory wooden table and four chairs stood in the middle of a floor covered in white tile. A leather sofa sat against the far wall, with a kitchen area opposite. There were no windows. Florescent lights hummed overhead and filled the room with a yellow hue.

Madelyn sat at the table, in silence, save for the TV mounted to the wall. It had been set to a local news station, and the story of the hour centered around protests on the University of Colorado's campus. She was used to being at the continual center of political activism, so Madelyn didn't think a story about marches at CU were newsworthy in the least. But since she had nothing else to do, she watched— seeing little and hearing less.

The door opened. Katarina entered. "I wish I had more to loan you." She held up a rose-colored, long-sleeved T-shirt. "But this is all I had on hand. You're welcome to it if you'd like a change of clothes."

"Thanks," said Madelyn, as she got up from her seat to accept the offered shirt. "I have to admit, wearing something clean will be nice."

"It's what I figured." Katarina pointed to a door that was tucked in next to the sofa. "You can change in there," she said.

Madelyn stepped into the half bath and closed the door before stripping out of her dirty and worn shirt and blazer. Water from the faucet sluiced between her fingers as she took time to wash her hands, face and neck. She toweled off with rough, industrial paper towels and redressed in the T-shirt.

Katarina waited by the table. "I also brought you this," she said, handing over a canvas bag.

Madelyn took it, again with her thanks, and tucked her dirty laundry inside.

"Can I get you anything else?" Katarina asked. "Something to drink? A sandwich?"

"A phone," said Madelyn. "I'd like to call my parents."

Katarina gave a sympathetic sigh. "Sorry. No can do. There's a lot of bigwigs who want to chat with you first."

"First?" Indignation and disbelief flamed inside of Madelyn's chest. "I've been waiting for almost forty minutes." She inhaled and exhaled, mastering her frustration at being thrown in a room and forgotten. She'd been all but discarded by Roman. Where was he?

"Roman's being debriefed right now," Katarina said, as if Madelyn's thoughts, and not the local news, were being broadcast on the TV. "I think he's almost done." A slim cell phone in Katarina's hand pinged and she looked at the screen. "In fact, he just wrapped up. Come with me."

I am a doctor. I am a doctor. I am a doctor, or will be one day. Madelyn repeated the phrase for confidence as she followed Katarina down a long hallway. Thick carpeting cushioned her steps and silenced her footfalls. Katarina stopped in front of a wooden door. A silver sign affixed to it read Conference Room A.

"Here you go, hon." The other woman opened the door. "All you need to do is answer a few questions. There's no need to worry."

Madelyn entered the room, her stomach bucking. A large wooden table sat in the middle of the floor. A bank of windows ran the span of the room and overlooked the Sixteenth Street Mall and the Denver skyline beyond. More than a dozen men and several women in dark suits or official uniforms sat around the table. To the person, their expressions were sour—as if they'd all sucked from the same rotten lemon.

The bright Rocky Mountain sun streamed through the windows and reflected off the highly polished table. The effect was blinding and slightly nauseated Madelyn, or maybe that symptom came from being nervous. The clean shirt notwithstanding, Madelyn didn't belong.

There was a single open chair at the foot of the table and Madelyn slid into the seat. Ian was at the head. Roman had changed into a white button-down shirt with the sleeves rolled up and charcoal slacks. He sat five seats up and on her right. He gave her a quick smile and lifted his hand in greeting. From where she sat, she could see the wording of his tattoo. *Hoc defendam. This we'll defend.* And for Madelyn, the words on his skin were true. He was her defender.

"Ms. Thompkins," Ian began. "Thank you for joining us. Allow me to make introductions." He rattled off names and agencies for every person in the room.

Madelyn would never remember them all. She didn't think she was supposed to, nor did she think she honestly had a choice in attending the meeting. "I'm happy to help," she said.

"We've been briefed by Mr. DeMarco," one man began. "But, in your own words, can you tell us what happened."

The thought of recounting everything that had happened felt like hiking across a sand dune—tiring, pointless, with one step forward becoming two steps back. And just like a hike over the dunes, Madelyn wanted this meeting to be over so she could go home.

"Roman's really thorough, so I'm not sure what you want. Do you have specific questions for me?"

The man who'd asked the original question held a pen. He cartwheeled it between his fingers and back. Madelyn thought Ian had said he was with the Federal Bureau of Investigation. "Mr. DeMarco claims that you came to the Boulder bar known as The Prow looking for your sister..."

It wasn't exactly a question, but rather an opening. "The last time I saw Ava was before she checked herself out of rehab. That was months ago. Last night, she posted something on social media and tagged herself as being at The Prow. I went to see if she was still there."

"Let's jump forward to today. Oleg Zavalov found the, up until now, hidden RMJ safe house."

Again, not a question. This time his words held a hint of blame. Madelyn's shoulder blades pinched together and the muscles in her lower back tightened. "Am I being accused of something?"

"Wait a minute," Roman interrupted. He was on his feet. "What are you implying?"

"Look at it from our perspective, Mr. DeMarco. Your case is blown on the night Ms. Thompkins arrives and then miraculously, Oleg Zavalov finds RMJ's safe house." Mr. FBI continued, "It doesn't add up."

Unfortunately, Madelyn could see the entire scenario from the FBI's perspective. There were several circumstances that didn't make sense, unless Oleg Zavalov had found out about Roman's investigation and then a way to infiltrate a spy.

"Roman must've told you that our lives were threatened by Oleg and his men," Madelyn said. "They were going to kill me."

"But they didn't."

She looked at Roman. He remained on his feet and glared at Mr. FBI. She thought about admitting to being Roman's lover. Then again, she might prove the point: Who beyond a spy involved in a honey trap would take a lover so quickly?

"Don't say anything else, Madelyn," Roman said as he sat. "You can ask for a lawyer if you want to." He pointed to Mr. FBI. "There are protocols to follow. If you want to question someone, you need to read them their rights. Ian, this is an ambush."

Roman glared at each man around the table. They all looked away. Finally, his gaze found hers and held for a moment. At least Roman believed her. What about Ian? He'd been so kind. Had it all been an act?

"This isn't an ambush," said Ian. "We have to examine this case from all angles. You know that, Roman. If you want a lawyer, just say so, Ms. Thompkins. We don't want you to feel as if your rights have been violated."

"I've got nothing to hide," Madelyn said, refusing to become a victim twice over. "I can prove that Ava is my sister, if that helps." She reached into her purse for her phone. She had dozens of pictures of them together from years gone by, and then there was the social media post. Madelyn hit the home button. The screen remained gray. She remembered too late that besides being out of battery, her phone had been submerged in the creek. She waved a weary hand. "It doesn't matter, you people could've found out that Ava's my sister by now if you wanted to."

"We have," said Mr. FBI. "And she is. We know that you're a med school student at CU and the fact that you're at the top of your class."

She was furious. "Wait a minute, you were looking into my academic records? Don't I have a right to my privacy?"

"I haven't told you anything that a nosy neighbor couldn't find out with a single social media account and half of an hour to waste. But rest assured, before I looked into your background, I received a judge's order."

Did she really care that the FBI verified her enrollment at the University of Colorado if it meant that they could catch a drug kingpin? "And what did you find?"

"Ms. Thompkins, your shopping habits don't really interest me. But I do have a theory. Your sister somehow runs awry of Oleg Zavalov and needs a favor to get back into his good graces. Around the time, he's starting to figure out that he has a mole who needs to be lured to light. He might even suspect Roman. If Ava can deliver, she's forgiven. There are only a few folks she can count on, one being you—her sister. You're a good person and willing to help."

She trusted these people to keep her, and everyone else, safe. But she didn't like Mr. FBI, even though his logic made sense. Maybe she'd been hasty in not accepting the offer for legal counsel. Then again, Mr. FBI was wrong. "That's not what happened. And even if it was, why did I shoot Oleg Zavalov when he found the safe house? What if I'd missed? Wouldn't that jeopardize my sister more?"

"You shot Oleg Zavalov?" Mr. FBI stopped twirling his pen.

He hadn't been told? She thought for sure that Roman filled them in on everything.

"Roman? I thought you shot Zavalov?" Ian had asked the question.

Roman looked at Madelyn and gave a small smile.

"I might have implied that fact, but I did it to protect Madelyn from further scrutiny."

Mr. FBI began twirling again. "So, when the gun fell during the altercation, you picked it up, Ms. Thompkins."

Another not-exactly-a-question kind of question. "I did and when Oleg lunged for me, I fired. I'm not quite sure where I hit him, but he fell in the creek."

"That part we know. Is there anything else you implied that wasn't exactly true, Mr. DeMarco?" Mr. FBI asked.

Roman shook his head. "Not a thing."

Mr. FBI tucked his pen into his shirtfront pocket. "If there are no other questions…"

She'd played their game, now it was time to get some help from them. "I have two questions for you. First, has anyone found my sister? And second, has Oleg Zavalov been located?"

A man in a dusty blue jacket of a Colorado Highway Patrol officer spoke. "As of now, Ava Thompkins hasn't broken any law, so there's no legal reason to pick her up. But we released an all-points bulletin asking our patrols to report any sightings."

"And Zavalov?"

"A search and rescue team has been deployed. As of now, his body has not been recovered."

"Body?"

"Or maybe I should clarify, he hasn't been found—dead or alive. Although as of now, we aren't expecting to find him alive."

"And if this is a recovery and not a rescue? Should I be worried about charges? Do I need a lawyer?" Madelyn asked.

Mr. FBI waved away her concern. "From everything I heard, it was self-defense, even when I thought it was Mr. DeMarco. If Colorado brings charges, let me know. I'll pay for your lawyer myself. And speaking of recovering bodies, unless there are objections, for now Serge's body remains hidden at The Prow. When the time comes, we'll bring in the Boulder PD, but we don't know how many officers can be trusted. Sounds as though at least one was Oleg's good friend." Jackson.

Madelyn liked Mr. FBI better, but only by a little.

"Now, unless there are any more questions." Mr. FBI paused and met Madelyn's gaze.

His look dared her to say more and just to be difficult, she considered doing exactly that. But when Mr. FBI continued, she was glad that she'd remained silent. "I say we adjourn and get to work. Ladies and gentlemen, we have one of the biggest drug dealers in the world to catch."

Chapter 8

Oleg's chest throbbed and numbness bit into his flesh. Sharp stones gouged his side and muddy water lapped at his legs. He opened his eyes, or rather eye. One was swollen shut. He pulled himself forward inch by painful inch, until he lay upon the sloping bank of the creek.

The sun shone overhead, warming his cold skin. He had no idea how long he'd floated in the cold water.

He sat up, gritting his teeth against the pain in his chest. He swore he'd been shot. He recalled the moment—the blast, the flash, the searing agony—with such clarity that his eyes watered.

With a featherlight touch, he explored the injury.

An angry, red bruise—the size of a deck of cards—had risen from his skin. It was directly beneath his phone. And then he understood. Madelyn had shot him—but his phone had absorbed the impact.

Oleg removed his jacket. A neat bullet hole had burrowed through the fabric of his breast pocket. His phone was dented, the screen shattered. He slipped the destroyed phone into the pocket of his pants and tossed the blazer back into the water.

Nikolai Mateev expected him this evening and Oleg had nothing to offer—no nephew, no money, no retribution. And now he couldn't even make a phone call or send a text. Oleg should've run when he had the chance. It had been naive to think that he could handle such a debacle as Serge being murdered. Hubris, his worst enemy, had gotten him in the end. Oleg spat, his spittle was full of dirt.

In the distance came the quiet humming of a motor, followed by the high-pitched scream of buffeted wind as a tractor trailer rumbled past. He rose to his knees, and then, gingerly, to his feet. He was drawn to the sound, which meant only one thing—a road. He hobbled upward; only wearing one shoe, shot in the chest, face swollen, suit ruined. The ridge crested, ending on the gravel-filled shoulder of a two-lane highway.

From the west came a humming, like a thousand angry bees, that belied another approaching tractor trailer. Oleg stepped into the middle of the road. This time he'd let fate decide. If the truck hit him, then he'd be no more dead than he was now. If it stopped, then Oleg was meant to live.

The white roof of the cab came into view first. Heat signatures rolled off the metal and smoky exhaust was caught in a slipstream of speed. The dual windshields grew large, nothing more than two blank eyes. The powerful air horn blared and the headlights flashed. One hundred yards between them and not enough room for a big rig to stop. Oleg swallowed down the last of his fear and regret. He closed his eyes and leaned back.

A screech of metal and the tar-filled stench of burning rubber wafted over Oleg. A door creaked open and then closed with a slam. It was followed by the sound of shoe leather slapping on asphalt.

"What are you doing out here?"

Fate had chosen. Oleg was saved. He opened his eyes to find a large African American man in a baseball cap and khaki shirt standing in the road. The name Buddy had been embroidered in red scroll over the right breast pocket.

"Hey man, can you hear me?" Buddy asked. "You don't look so good."

"My car was stolen," Oleg said, "and I was beaten, shot and thrown in the creek." None of what he said had been a lie. At the same time, Oleg felt that with a story such as his, Buddy would feel obligated to help.

"What is the world coming to? All of that pain for a car?"

"It was quite a car," Oleg said.

"Even an expensive car doesn't make it right," Buddy said. "Get in the cab, I can radio the sheriff."

"No sheriff," Oleg said quickly.

Buddy scratched his chin and slowly shook his head. "I'm not used to breaking any laws. But I'm also not going to leave you stranded out here." He shrugged. "Whatever happened, you need help. Get in. The least I can do is give you a lift."

Oleg worked his way into the cab and settled on the vinyl seat. The satellite radio was set to a gospel station and a crucifix hung from the rearview mirror. Fate had even delivered to him a godly man. Buddy jumped into the seat next to Oleg and put the semi truck into gear. They slowly climbed the hill and their speed increased on the descent.

"I guess I should thank you for the ride," Oleg said. Maybe it was the low tones of country music filling the cab that left him so appreciative.

"Never ignore a stranger in need," said Buddy. "It's my life's motto."

Since the truck driver was feeling so generous, perhaps he would take Oleg back to Boulder. Now that he'd been spared, Oleg knew he needed to live. First order of business: break all ties with the Mateev organization.

Discarding his goal of becoming an important person left him hollow—a mere shell of himself. Besides, he didn't need the Mateevs to advance his life anymore. Oleg had gotten this far on his own wiles.

Plus, he did have a good bit of Nikolai's money hidden at The Prow.

"If you can get me to Boulder," Oleg said to Buddy, "I can make it worth your while."

"I won't ignore a stranger in need and I won't take money that I didn't earn."

Buddy's seemingly simple rules for life were becoming more and more complex.

"If you took me to Boulder, then you would've earned your fee."

The other man shook his head. "I'm not going to Boulder, but I'll drop you off at the truck stop that's up the road a few miles ahead. I've only got a twenty-dollar bill in my pocket, but it's yours."

Oleg opened his mouth to argue. Buddy held up a hand the size of a dinner plate. "Don't argue with me about it, either. My mind's set."

Oleg closed his mouth and looked out the window.

"I'll also give you a jacket to cover up your messy shirt. You can't walk around with all that blood and gore if you don't want the sheriff called."

"Thanks," said Oleg.

"I'm just happy the zombie apocalypse hasn't started because that's what I thought when I first saw you." Buddy gave a long and loud laugh.

Oleg couldn't help but smile a little. Pain ripped at his lip. "I'm not that bad."

"Not that bad? You look like the walking dead, man."

Within minutes, Buddy pulled into the truck stop.

He gave Oleg the promised twenty and jacket that was four sizes too big. For good measure, Buddy threw in a pair of flip-flops meant for a giant, so at least Oleg had two huge shoes.

Slap. Slap. Slap. Oleg walked slowly from the gas pumps to the travel plaza, unsure of his next move. He gazed longingly at each car he passed. Jealous of those with transportation—like a spurned lover at a Valentine's dance during a slow song. He stopped next to the bumper of a dirt-covered luxury sedan. It was the same make and model as his, but it couldn't be his car, could it?

He read the license plate. He read it again. What were the chances that Roman and Madelyn would simply abandon his car in this lot?

He quickly looked over his shoulder. Oleg saw no one. He reached into the wheel well and found what he was looking for: a magnetic box that held his spare key. He unlocked the door and slipped into the driver's seat.

Not long ago, he'd worried that pride was his greatest fault. Now he knew better. Oleg put the car in gear and drove toward the interstate. Hubris was not his enemy. Oleg won because he was better than everyone else, and it was about time the world came to understand that valuable truth.

Madelyn stood next to the long bank of windows and looked down seventeen stories to the pedestrian mall below. It was lunchtime and business people in suits talked on phones as they hurried to meetings that included a meal. A teacher led a large group of children on a school trip through the historic downtown.

Madelyn felt the distance from humanity as a loss, not a sanctuary. Those gathered had recently departed, but the debris of their meeting remained. There were a half dozen water glasses and coffee cups scattered about the conference table, along with forgotten pens and unused legal pads.

She heard a noise from behind, just a slight breath of movement, and knew immediately it was Roman. Maybe it was that he brought with him the scent of their time in the cabin, or maybe her heart simply shared his beat. Without turning around, she spoke. "What just happened?"

"You were tested and passed," he said.

Tested? "I usually like to study before being quizzed. Or at least know that I'm taking an exam, especially one that is a total grilling."

"Like I said before, I didn't know that Special Agent Jones was going to go after you. If I had known... They have to explore every possibility..." He sighed. "I'm sorry. It's a federal offense to threaten an FBI agent, but I did want to choke Jones. You held your own, though."

She turned to look at Roman. In this light, his hazel eyes were jade green—like those in an exotic sculpture. "I took the MCATs. I don't intimidate easily."

He chuckled. "No, you don't."

Roman stood next to her. He braced his arms on the windowsill and looked down. She glanced at his profile and her breath caught in her chest. He was amazingly handsome. No wonder she'd taken him as a temporary lover. The one thing she hadn't anticipated was the heartache that would come with his departure from her life.

"I want to go home," she said.

"You will, as soon as Nikolai Mateev arrives and arrests are made. Until he's in custody, you won't be safe."

"If Oleg Zavalov is dead, then I have nothing to worry about. This Mateev guy never knew anything about me, so he's no threat."

"I'll see what I can do about a police officer staying with you. Or better yet, you can hang out here for a couple of hours."

A couple of hours? It felt like a month. With a shake of her head, Madelyn said, "I just need to get back to my normal life."

"Honestly, you're jeopardizing the entire case. I know this has all been horrible for you, but you can be patient for a few more hours. If not for your own safety, then think of the greater good."

That was just it; meeting Roman, spending time with him, being with him—none of that had been horrible. And still, she need to leave.

"Am I under arrest?" she asked.

"Of course not."

"Then I can go whenever I want?"

"Sure."

"I'm leaving now, then."

Madelyn turned from the window, sweat trickling down her back. Roman gripped her arm, stopping her. She refused to look at him.

"If you're sure that you want to go home, I'll take you."

"Don't bother." She tried to jerk her arm away. He didn't let go.

There was a hollowness in her chest that threatened to implode, leaving a gaping chasm that would fill with nothing but sorrow and loneliness. They weren't destined to be together, so why prolong the inevitable?

"I insist," he said, his voice was low and husky.

The hairs on Madelyn's arm lifted, a reaction to his sultry voice and strong touch. Their eyes met and her mouth went dry.

She wanted to kiss him. She wanted to slap him. She didn't want to relent. And yet, she only wanted to give in.

"Fine," she said, pulling away hard. His grip broke. Arms folded tightly across her chest, chin tucked down, Madelyn left the conference room at a quick clip. Each step down the hall showed disdain for Roman and his suggestion that she cared only for herself.

Even if his words rang just a bit true.

Roman jogged after her. "The garage is this way." He pointed to a corridor she'd just stalked past.

It was difficult to hold on to her anger when she was chagrined. Madelyn shook her head and sighed. She no longer had the strength for a fight. "You lead, I'll follow."

They rounded a corner and Katarina came into view. She chatted with a receptionist who sat behind a half-circle desk of steel and glass. The wall behind was filled with a backlit trio of interconnected letters: RMJ.

"Kat," Roman said as they entered the reception area. "I'm going to take Madelyn back to Boulder. I'll look at the phones found in Zavalov's car when I get back."

Katarina screwed her lips to the side. "Sorry, hon. Special Agent Jones took the phones with him."

"What? Are you kidding me? I can get into the phones faster than the FBI's IT guys can."

"You have other things to worry about right now," Katarina said.

Madelyn wondered if one of those concerns was supposed to be her.

Then Katarina wrapped her arm around Madelyn's shoulder, drawing her in. "Take care of yourself and good luck with school. We need more good doctors in the world."

"Thanks," said Madelyn, unsure what else she should say when all she wanted to do was go home. "For everything," she finally thought to add.

"Oh, and you left these in the break room." From

behind the reception desk, Katarina produced the canvas bag filled with Madelyn's soiled laundry.

"I have your shirt on," Madelyn said, suddenly feeling as if she owed Katarina more than just her thanks.

"You keep it. The color suits you."

This time when Katarina moved in for a hug, Madelyn wrapped her arms around the older woman's shoulders and pulled her into an embrace.

Madelyn went numb. She didn't recall the rest of the short walk to the parking garage or even finding Roman's car. Yet they had and she found herself in the passenger seat of a quasi tank like the one in which Ian had collected them. Roman's SUV, however, was a steely blue. Out of the parking garage. Out of Denver. Onto the interstate to Boulder. The sun heated the car and she set her tote bag in the back seat. As the miles slipped away, so did Madelyn's anger, leaving her simply sad that she and Roman would part ways. Once in Boulder, Madelyn gave Roman directions to her apartment. He parked in the space reserved for her lost car.

"You know me well enough to know that there's no use in you telling me that I can't walk you to your apartment. Remember, I was an Eagle Scout," he said with a grin.

Her middle flip-flopped at his smile and her cheeks warmed with a blush. Did she know Roman well? If she didn't believe in love at first sight, only pheromones and serotonin, why did she feel as if she'd known Roman her whole life? Or maybe it wasn't that she knew him well, but rather understood him.

She looked at her apartment building. An open stairwell climbed up four floors and her door was visible, even from the car. It all seemed different, but at the same time, it was just as she had left it. Or perhaps it was she who had changed. Like she'd been living in a fairy tale, the events of the past day were too fantastic to believe, both good and bad. For once in her life, Madelyn liked the notion of being the beautiful princess in need of rescuing.

"I guess this is where I thank you for being my knight in shining armor."

"You know you can call me whenever you need anything, Madelyn."

Was there an invitation in his words? Did he want to see her again? Would he ask her out on another date?

She held her breath and waited for him to continue. He didn't. Yet, she knew he wouldn't. She'd rejected him before he could reject her. At the time, it had made sense. And now? Well, now Madelyn didn't know what to think.

So, it was goodbye from him, too. She told herself that she didn't mind and it truly was for the best. Their relationship consisted of the briefest of moments and not a lifetime of shared experiences. Still her eyes burned with unshed tears and a knot clogged her throat. "Well, I better…" Her words trailed off.

She stepped out of the car, and with that ended

whatever magic was in the air. The asphalt underfoot radiated heat collected from the sun. She began to sweat and, at the same time, shiver.

Roman was out of the car and at her side. "Forty-six B," he said. "Right?"

Madelyn paused, surprised that he would know her apartment number without her ever having shared it. Then again, RMJ and the federal government knew everything about her.

She nodded and led him to the correct stairwell, then up four flights of stairs to her door. A brass letter *B* hung on the wall. She unzipped her purse, a little surprised that she hadn't lost it in all the excitement, and dug through the contents.

No key.

In that instant, it was all too much. All her defenses tumbled to the ground, like a set of wooden building blocks in the hands of a child having a tantrum. Her emotions spilled over.

Roman wrapped her in his arms. He shushed her, his breath washing over her hair. "I can get the door open for you, then I'll get a new key made." His tone, more than his words, was soothing.

Madelyn hiccupped as the seemingly endless stream of tears abated. "Okay," she said, wiping hard at both eyes. "I'm okay. I have a spare key in the apartment."

"Let's just get you inside and we can take it from there."

We. She thrilled at the thought of togetherness, of

not having to finish this nightmare alone. Roman's arms remained around her waist. Her head was still tucked into his chest. She wanted to stay like that forever, but she knew she couldn't. Years before, she had chosen a path and it was time to rediscover her original trail.

"Thanks for getting me into my apartment," she said.

Roman stepped away from their embrace. Kneeling before the door, he examined the lock. "Do you remember if you engaged the dead bolt?"

Before she could try to remember, much less answer, Roman turned the handle. The door swung silently open.

"It's open? I could've sworn that I locked my door. I always do…" Her words trailed off.

"It's okay," he said. Roman's embrace was the only thing keeping Madelyn from a full-blown panic attack.

He released his hold. "Wait here for a minute. I'm going to check out your apartment."

Roman nudged the door open and stepped inside. After a moment, he motioned her forward. "Is there anything wrong with your apartment? Anything misplaced or missing?"

Madelyn stepped into her apartment and looked around. Textbooks still sat in a pile on her breakfast bar. Her TV, a Christmas gift from her parents, remained on the stand. Dishes from dinner two nights ago sat in a strainer, yesterday's breakfast dishes were unwashed in the sink. "It's exactly as I left it, although it's not like me to leave the door unlocked. Maybe from the beginning, yesterday had been wrong."

Roman steered her to the sofa and opened the patio blinds. Sun streamed into the room, catching dust motes as they swirled around, suddenly awakened by her return.

"Do you mind if I look around?" Roman asked. "You can't be too careful."

She wasn't sure what he expected to find. Then again, that was the point. He was an expert, she was just a girl who hoped to one day be a doctor. She swept her arm across her body, encompassing the dining-living room combo. "Feel free."

Roman took his time. He opened every cabinet and looked in each drawer. It was all as it should be. For the first time in a day, she began to feel relaxed. She slumped on the sofa and watched Roman as he entered her bedroom. As the tension and panic faded from her body, she began to feel exhaustion take over, and her tired gaze roamed the room as she longed to put her head on a pillow and—

She sat bolt upright, staring at the wall next to the TV. Light shone on the paint, illuminating a faint discoloration where a photo had hung. Like a magnet, her eyes were drawn to the coffee table before her.

Atop a pile of binders and papers sat the photo.

The picture was of Ava and Madelyn at a Fourth of July barbecue following Ava's first stint in rehab. That moment, caught by their mother's camera, was one of the happiest in Madelyn's life. Her sister had sunk to the depths of hell, but like a phoenix she'd risen from the ashes of addiction. At that time, Madelyn believed that her sister had been cured and from then on, her family would always be blessed.

Madelyn had been wrong—as wrong as it was for that picture to be set aside on the table, and not on the wall. Her heartbeat stilled.

"Roman." Even in her own ears she heard the panic in her voice.

He stood in the doorway that separated her bedroom from the rest of the apartment. "What's the matter?"

Madelyn swallowed. "I think that Oleg's been in my apartment."

Knowing that Oleg Zavalov had been in her home left Madelyn feeling dirty. Violated. Like his filthy hands had somehow touched her. She wondered what in her apartment he had fondled. Her food? Her books? Her underwear? She might have to throw everything away and start over.

"How do you know?"

"That photo is usually on the wall."

Roman sat beside her. "He's not here now," he said. "We know that because he's somewhere downstream from the safe house, maybe his body has even made it to the Colorado River by now. But, I'm calling in a CSI team."

She didn't want more people in her home. With a shake of her head, Madelyn said, "Forget it. I don't want anyone else in my house. I just need to get over all of this." She was quiet for a moment. "Is it awful for me to be glad he's dead?"

Roman sat next to her and lifted her feet into his lap. "With him gone, you have the ultimate security. So it's not wrong to be happy that you're safe."

Madelyn licked her lips and nodded.

"Let me make you a cup of tea. It's the best medicine." Roman rose and walked to the kitchen. He found the kettle on the stove, picked it up and started filling it with water. Madelyn saw the scene all too clearly; them together and Roman's endearing notion that tea somehow solved all the world's ills. Or maybe it was just the care that he put into the cup. But being together wasn't in their future. They'd already decided. No, really it was she who had decided long ago when she'd dedicated herself to her studies and her future career.

Playing house was not a game for her.

"I'm okay," she said, raising her voice to be heard over the running tap.

Roman turned off the water, a finger to his ear.

"I'm okay," she repeated, knowing all the while it was a lie. Madelyn wouldn't be okay for a very long time to come. But she needed to reclaim her life and now seemed as good a time as any. "You don't have to worry about making me tea. I think I'll get cleaned up and rest. I should probably get in touch with my parents and let them know what's going on with Ava."

Roman paused and glanced at the teapot in his hand, as if he wasn't sure what to do with it. Or maybe he wasn't sure what to do with her. "I can stay until you get settled…"

"I'm as settled as I'm going to be. If I need someone I'll call a friend."

"I'm your friend," he said.

"You know what I mean. I can call someone I know."

"You know me."

"Not really," she said with a shake of her head. "I wouldn't have survived without you over the past twenty-four or so hours. But, we don't know each other."

"We can get to know each other better."

"How?"

Roman said, "We can talk, like normal people do."

"About what?"

"Okay, what's your favorite color?" he asked.

"That's juvenile," she said. "You should stop now."

"I wish you'd stop lecturing me like I'm a dumb student who can't pass a test," he said.

"I work hard and I'm sorry that I don't have lots of spare time to swap stories about our favorite colors or if we liked our second-grade teacher or not. But I have a life plan and that plan does not include you."

She hadn't meant to be so direct. In fact, she hadn't meant to say what she'd said, but she couldn't figure out a way to take her words back. "I'm sorry," she began.

"Sure," Roman said. He set the kettle on the counter.

"No, really, I'm sorry..."

"Don't apologize," he said. "I get it and I should've gotten it before. You've been straight with me about your priorities from the beginning. It's just that when I see something I want, I go after it. I'm sure there's some kind of biochemical brain–emotional transference rationale to explain my behavior. I'm sure you understand whatever's happened to me all too well."

"Don't leave while you're mad."

"I'm not mad," he said, "but I really should leave. And if I hear anything about Ava, I'll call."

"But I have to get a new phone and I don't know what my new number will be..."

"I'll find it."

Of course he would.

"If there's nothing else..." he said.

Stay, her mind screamed. *Ask him to stay. Insist— and then step into his embrace. It's the safest place on earth.* "I'm good," she said.

Roman paused and then, with a nod, he left. The door closed. The latch fell into place and Madelyn jolted. She jumped from the sofa and sprinted across the floor. Breathless, she reached for the door handle. Her fingers grazed the cold metal and she stopped. She liked Roman, cared for him deeply. But she had to ask herself, was she willing to throw away all her hard work and sacrifice just to be with him?

Her heartbeat raced, her pulse thrumming at the base of her throat. She didn't know and in a way, that was an answer.

Roman stood on the threshold, his forehead pressed into the door. He should knock. He should go back in. Then what? She'd sent him away once already. He wasn't going to beg someone to love him—even though he was tempted. Roman inhaled, filling the empty space in his chest with a deep breath.

Still miserable, he walked away.

Next to his car, he stood by the door and looked up at Madelyn's apartment. There was a deck attached to her living room. He made a bet with himself—if she cared enough to come to the door and watch him leave, it meant that their time together was something more than pure survival—and he would return to her apartment. He watched the patio and the sliding glass door beyond. It was a blank face with a mouth full of spindly teeth.

The late afternoon sun was brilliant, and reflected off the hood of his car. His eyes watered and he wiped them with his shoulder.

He gave one more look to Madelyn's patio. It was still empty.

Roman never made a bet, even in his own head, and he bit back a curse for being so gullible. Getting behind the wheel of his car, he drove out of the parking lot. He took turns using instinct more than thought and soon, was on the interstate heading south. He turned on the radio's news station and listened to the live coverage from the protests on the University of Colorado's campus. But he soon found it difficult to focus and turned the radio off. He had problems of his own—Madelyn, his heart said. But his mind knew there were other important issues, namely the apprehension of the biggest drug dealer in the world.

He had to admit, it felt good to be in action again. His pulse was strong and steady. His vision was clear, his mind sharp. Just like his days in Delta Force when Roman had been the point of the spear. And this time, he had hit Nikolai Mateev with deadly accuracy. Maybe he'd be able to help with the arrest. That is, if they could figure out when and where Nikolai would be arriving.

A roadside sign indicated that Roman's exit was several miles ahead. Traffic surrounded him on all sides. Ready to change lanes, he turned on the blinker and glanced in the rearview mirror. But his gaze didn't travel to the road, rather it landed on a canvas tote bag with Madelyn's soiled clothes. He remembered Katarina handing it over before leaving the RMJ offices. He considered turning around, discarded the idea and thought about it again.

Like it was meant to be, a space opened in the right lane, and Roman changed lanes. Another exit, one he could use to head north and back to Boulder, was ahead. Certainly, Madelyn would want her clothes returned to her. Wouldn't she? Or maybe not. He could have them mailed.

He growled. "Damn."

His analytical skills were failing him. Yet, before he could decide what to do, the phone rang. Using the steering wheel's control to answer the call, Roman said, "Hello?"

"Where are you?" Ian asked.

"Getting off the highway. What's up?"

"We've just gotten word that a private jet is about to land at DIA."

Denver International Airport was one of the busiest in the world. No doubt thousands of private flights landed each day, there had to be more. "Is it Nikolai Mateev's?"

"There's evidence that it is. It originated in Moscow, stopping only in Victoria, British Columbia, to refuel."

"It's the same route that Mateev's attorney Peter Belkin planned to use if he'd been successful in kidnapping Nikolai's grandson over Christmas," Roman said. RMJ had been instrumental in saving four-year-old Gregory Mateev from being taken from the country and raised by his gangster grandfather in Russia. Intel from that case had been cornerstone for the one Roman had built at The Prow.

"I made the same connection," said Ian.

A question returned to Roman, one that he had asked himself before, but never posed to anyone else.

"Why?"

"Why, what?"

"Why is Nikolai Mateev going to all of this trouble? First there was the kidnapping of his grandson and the attempted murder of the boy's mother. If both hadn't been botched, the grandkid would be in Russia. I guess I understand that Nikolai might want to raise his grandson after his own son died. But Serge? He's what? A great-nephew? And if Nikolai wants a family reunion, why not make Serge go to Russia?"

"The reports we have from Sledkom state that Serge was wanted in Russia."

Roman had read the same reports coming from the Russian equivalent to the American FBI. "Okay, so Serge can't go back to Moscow, but why would Nikolai come *here*? Why America? And why Colorado, in particular? What's here that he needs?"

"That's a good question," said Ian, "and if you hurry, you can meet us at the private terminal and ask him yourself."

Roman glanced once more at the tote bag in his back seat, sorry that timing hadn't been right. He stepped on the accelerator, passing the exit and heading to the airport.

Madelyn fluffed her hair with a towel and wandered to the living room. Beyond taking a shower, she didn't know what to do. Study? Eat? She had little appetite and her mind still raced with the events of the last day, taking with it the ability to focus.

She shouldn't have kicked Roman out of her life. Beyond being handsome, brave, smart and funny, he was, well, perfect. For too long, Madelyn had told herself that it was her studies that kept her alone. Yet in her heart of hearts, Madelyn knew it was the rejection from her last boyfriend that she carried around, like a heavy stone.

But other people's relationships ended every day. They cried, ate ice cream, cried, joined a yoga class and got back into dating. Not Madelyn. She'd constructed a cocoon of protection around her life, insisting that she couldn't come out, lest she ruin her chances to become a butterfly. Her theory held a measure of truth, but only the smallest amount.

Mindlessly, she picked up the photo of her and Ava. Could it be, as Madelyn sometimes worried, that she hadn't been a good enough sister to keep Ava off drugs. What if Madelyn was somehow the cause?

As soon as Madelyn acknowledged the thought, she knew it wasn't true. Sure, she was imperfect, but she wasn't a horrible person—someone only to be tolerated through the haze of self-medication. The thought was freeing and at the same time, the realization came too late. Roman was gone. She'd blown her chance at happiness, and now Madelyn had no choice but to remain in her cocoon.

She needed to speak to someone who would offer her sympathy. Her parents. They should know what happened to her, and that Ava was somewhere in

Boulder. Even though her phone was ruined, she should be able to text with her computer.

Flopping down on the sofa with her laptop, Madelyn hit the power button. Her screen lit up, with an illuminated tool bar at the bottom. Her text bubble had seventeen unread messages. She scrolled through them, giving each one a halfhearted read. Belatedly, she realized that she'd never asked Roman for his number. It was an oversight, to be sure. At the same time, he'd never offered.

She returned to the texts. Offers to join friends for dinner. Questions about notes from classmates. And Ava. Seven words, the first she'd seen from her sister in months.

I need help. Come and get me.

That text was followed by another with a Boulder street address.

Maddie? she had asked.

And then: Are you there?

Finally: Why are you ignoring me?

Ava. The person who let Madelyn climb in bed during thunderstorms. Ava. The first person to predict that Madelyn would become a doctor. Ava. The one who held Madelyn as she cried when her best friend in fifth grade found a better best friend. Ava. The one who took medication from their parents' bathroom and washed it down with whiskey stolen from the liquor cabinet, but then dumped a wine cooler that Madelyn had poured into a plastic cup at a family picnic. Ava. The one who said she never felt right in her own skin and just needed to escape. But how do you escape from yourself?

I need help. Come and get me.

I'm here, Madelyn typed. Anything you need.

She hit Send and her text moved into the conversation. Delivered.

Madelyn looked back at Ava's texts. They had been sent starting at 5:06 AM.

It was now almost six o'clock in the evening Almost a whole day was gone. What had Madelyn been doing at that exact moment? She knew. She'd been asleep, lying in Roman's arms, without a care in the world. And her sister?

I need help. Come and get me.

Drugs. Alcohol. Life on the streets. What kind of terror had Ava faced? What could Madelyn have done to make it better?

The text field changed from blank to having three dots. Her sister was replying.

Oleg parked down the block and stared at the front door of The Prow. He watched for signs that the place was under surveillance. Aside from his car, there were no conspicuously parked autos. More than that, no coroner's wagon was at the curb. No crime scene tape covered the door. No cops, with boxes full of evidence, striding in and out of the building.

Madelyn Thompkins was just as she appeared—a

medical school student with crappy timing. But Oleg didn't know what to make of Roman Black. Right before Oleg went in the water, Roman had spoken of justice. Which meant what if no police waited at The Prow?

He put the car in gear and circled the block, parking beside the basement stairs. He'd watched Roman for months and never saw a misstep. In fact, Oleg came to trust him.

Had he been wrong? Like a snake eating its own tail, Oleg came back to his original question. If it wasn't Roman who'd bugged his office, then who?

Serge and Anton? What would they gain by double-crossing Oleg, unless they were after the money that Oleg laundered for Nikolai? In bringing down two cheats, could Oleg find a way to remain relevant with Nikolai Mateev? Oleg's hands trembled with the possibility that he need not abandon his life's plan.

He entered the back door of The Prow and went first to the beer cooler. Anton and Serge still lay on the metal floor. The hallway was still filled with blood. Without question, no one had been in The Prow since Oleg left.

Oleg's mind changed again and again. Stay. Go. Face Nikolai. Disappear. It was best, he decided, to prepare for any eventuality. And that meant he had to collect the money hidden at the back of the bar. And then what? The sharp trill of his office phone ringing interrupted Oleg's thoughts. He sprinted across the hall and lifted the handset from the cradle. "Hello?" he said, breathless.

"Oleg?" It was a woman, her voice weak and scratchy. A junkie, too feeble to speak. He didn't have time to waste and pulled the phone from his ear, ready to hang up. "It's Ava," the woman whispered, "Ava Thompkins. It's about my sister, Madelyn."

Oleg exhaled. Was it worthwhile to pursue Madelyn Thompkins? Well, she had shot him and as far as Oleg was concerned, that was a deed that could not go unpunished.

"Have you heard from her?"

"Finally," said Ava. "But I'm sick. I need more medicine from you."

She meant heroin, the only thing that would ease her pain short of death's icy kiss. He had plenty of drugs on hand, more even than the ten baggies he'd tempted her with. "If you can deliver your sister, I'll give you the full amount."

"I think she's at home."

"I don't want you to guess, I need to know where she is. Better yet, get her to meet you somewhere."

"I'll text her." A pause. "She wants to know if I'm still at the address I texted about this morning."

"Are you?"

"No."

"Find out if she's alone." Oleg needed to know if he'd be dealing with just Madelyn or if he would be forced to face Roman again.

"She says she is."

The perfect plan came to Oleg. All he needed was to get Madelyn back to The Prow. He doubted that she would be dumb enough to return to the bar, even if her sister asked. What Oleg needed was to take Madelyn by complete surprise.

"Tell her to meet you at the University Memorial Center. Second-floor study lounge."

The University of Colorado's student union was perfect. Not only would Madelyn feel completely safe in such a public place, the second-floor lounge was rarely used. Except by people like Oleg. He had passed on drugs for money many times in that room without ever being bothered. This time, he'd need backup and help. With Serge and Anton both dead, Oleg was shorthanded. He could call Jackson, never mind that the cop had threatened to sever all ties.

"She wants to know when?" Ava asked.

Oleg could get to the university in fifteen minutes, but he'd need to get ready. He reached into his pocket for his cell. He drew out the dented hunk of metal and plastic that used to be his phone.

"What time is it now?" Oleg asked.

"Six-oh-four," Ava said.

"Tell her to meet you at half past the hour. And you need to be there, too."

"No way. I don't know what you want with Madelyn, but she's my sister. I can't let her know that I'm involved."

Ava really was high if she thought Madelyn wouldn't figure out it was her sister who had set her up. "You want your drugs? Be at the Memorial Center in fifteen minutes and do exactly as I say."

Ava exhaled, her voice even weedier than before. "I'll text her." Then, a moment later, "O, M, W," Ava said.

"What?"

"That's her reply. On my way."

Chapter 9

The plane, a Bombardier Challenger 300, touched down on the runway at Denver International Airport, the last rays of sun glinted off the fuselage.

Behind the plane came a cadre of cars and SUVs. Sirens blaring and lights flashing, the official vehicles surrounded the aircraft. It was forced to a remote hangar, where a battalion's worth of law enforcement officials waited. Adrenaline surged through Roman's veins. One gun in hand, another in a holster on his thigh, body armor over his chest and tactical glasses to protect his eyes—it was Roman's favorite outfit.

The aircraft's stairs were lowered.

"Out of the plane!"

The two passengers—both male—disembarked

from the Bombardier Challenger's cabin, which was large enough to hold twenty. Both men descended the stairs, hands raised. Even without the private charter jet, Roman would have recognized them as wealthy. They wore thick gold watches and heavy gold chains, along with Italian leather loafers and skinny jeans so tight they looked shiny—and most likely European. But without question, neither man was Nikolai Mateev.

On the other hand, they weren't simply business-men. Traveling under bogus passports, they had a plane full of black market clothing. Not exactly the head of the Russian Mafia, but the men were break-ing some serious laws.

Roman and Ian stood a little to the side as Special Agent Jones from the FBI called Customs to come and take custody of the plane and its contents.

"A little less than what we expected," said Ian. Even under his body armor, he wore a white button-down shirt and tie.

"Which means that Nikolai Mateev could be any-where."

"We'd been so sure..." Ian's words trailed off as another RMJ operative, Cody Samuels, approached.

"Ian," Cody said as he extended his hand in greet-ing. And then added, "Roman," as he turned to shake hands again. "I have some news you all might find interesting. First, the task force is reconvening in half an hour at the FBI's Denver field office."

"We'll be there," said Ian.

Roman's mind was well beyond the next strategic meeting. "You think this is a stunt? It was easy to find these guys and figure out that things weren't right. It could be that we were meant to find them, so they were dangled into our view. Like a magician's sleight of hand."

"You think they're decoys?" asked Cody.

"Could be."

"It's a theory worth considering," said Ian.

Roman scanned the empty hangar, nothing more than a domed metal roof and concrete floor. He searched every inch, as if Nikolai Mateev was hiding nearby and laughing his butt off.

"What makes it worse," Cody continued, "is that the car you recovered from Zavalov was stolen before we could pick it up."

"Stolen?" Roman's ears buzzed, like the word itself had damaged his hearing.

"A highway patrol unit went out to pick it up and it was gone."

"Do they have video from the truck stop?"

Cody shook his head. "Not a second of it. It was parked in a location that just missed surveillance. We do have tape of it driving away, but no clear view of the driver."

Roman had been so careful about where he'd parked, not wanting either Madelyn or himself filmed. His wonderful plan had backfired.

Cody continued. "Until the car is recovered, no one can collect any evidence."

The buzzing in Roman's ear grew until every part of his body itched. Much like when the plane landed, adrenaline flooded his system. Only this time it didn't leave him powerful and ready for battle, rather it left him detached as he watched events he wasn't completely a part of. "And what about Oleg Zavalov?" he asked Cody. "Has his body been recovered?"

"Not yet, although he could be halfway to the state line by now. He'll turn up, though. They always do."

Roman had parked his SUV at the back of the hangar. Without a word, he took off at a trot. It could all be just as Cody predicted. A nice car abandoned in the truck stop would be a prime target for thieves. And the mountain streams would rage and roil for weeks to come. Since Oleg hadn't surfaced quickly, he might not rise ever again. But still, like the two black marketers, it all seemed too simple.

And Madelyn was alone. There were too many loose threads for him to feel comfortable with her not having protection—provided by him.

"Roman!" His name echoed in the empty hangar.

He turned. Ian chased after him. Roman slowed and walked backward.

"Are you heading to the FBI's office?"

Roman shook his head. "I'm going back to Boulder. I have something to drop off at Madelyn's."

Madelyn took RTD, Boulder's public transportation system, to the University of Colorado's main campus. The hospital, where she spent most of her time, was miles from the redbrick buildings of the college's center. It's not that Madelyn never came to campus, she did. But what she found was wholly unexpected and left her breathless.

The central lawn was packed with people. From a distance, she wondered if it was an end of semester concert, but as she approached, Madelyn saw the protest signs and banners rising from the crowd, a field of flowers springing up from the grassroots of humanity. This was the rally from earlier news reports.

A dais had been constructed outside an administrative building. Several students filled the platform. A young man, with a sparse goatee and frayed denim jacket, stood behind a podium. His voice was carried by a string of speakers held on poles around the perimeter of the crowd. He challenged leadership to explain the most recent tuition increase. "Come on down," he said, his voice taking on the singsong quality of a game show host.

Madelyn left the crowd behind, thankful that Ava had suggested they meet at the Memorial Center. She needed a quiet place to talk to her sister. Assuming the protest remained peaceful, a study lounge would give them the solitude they needed. Hope rose within Madelyn's chest. Did Ava need help? Was she ready for a change?

Pushing open a heavy glass door, Madelyn entered the student union. The main floor, consisting of a coffee shop, study area, fireplace and TV lounge, was empty. Even the cafeteria was closed. Her footfalls on the tile floor echoed through the vast space. She headed to the winding stairwell that led to the second floor.

She peered through a window, inset in the door. The room beyond was dark as pitch. She reread the plastic nameplate attached to the wall. Second Floor Study Lounge. She looked into the room again, this time she saw the faint outline of a person sitting on a chair.

Madelyn opened the door. A light, controlled by a motion detector, came on. The person in the chair was Ava, unquestionably Ava, but not. She was thinner than even Madelyn had guessed from the social media photo and she still wore the same dirty shirt from that night. Ava's collarbones cut sharply out of the stretched neck. An open sore on her cheek, angry and red, was a stark contrast to her pale skin. Dark hair hung in lank clumps past her shoulders.

Her sister's head lolled to the side. Her eyes were shut. A white, powdery residue ringed her nose.

Madelyn also saw her playmate and best friend from years gone by. Brown eyes, so much like her own, twinkling with fun and mischief. A secret whispered on a summer's night, carried away by a hot breeze. Snowball fights. Exciting first dates. Bad breakups.

Madelyn knelt at Ava's side. She touched her sister's arm and shook lightly. "Ava, it's me, Maddie."

Nothing. She looked around the space, taking it

in for the first time. The upholstered chair was one of a dozen that sat around the edge of the room. A table stood to the side, surrounded by half a dozen straight-backed chairs. Another door, to the left, was closed. The room beyond was dark, and most likely set aside for students to prepare presentations. She searched the walls for a phone and found none. Madelyn needed to find help for her sister, and at the same time, she was loath to leave Ava's side when she'd found her only moments before.

"Hey." Madelyn shook her sister's arm again and tried to think of the best plan—take Ava to her house or get her straight to CU Hospital's detox unit? For the first time in her life, she wanted another person with whom she could share her burdens. She wanted Roman. It was a futile desire. Beyond her crazy-busy life, Madelyn now had Ava to take care of and she had to save Ava from, well, Ava. She couldn't ask Roman to tether himself to such a heavy weight.

Ava blinked. "Hey."

Madelyn laughed, their greeting a comedy of the absurd, and wiped the tears from her cheeks. "Ava," she began, "it's so good to see you. You don't know how worried I've been—how worried Mom and Dad have been. It doesn't matter. I'm here now."

She reached for her sister. Ava shrank back. Madelyn's hand hung, suspended in midair, like a speech bubble over a cartoon—empty except for a question mark.

"I'm sorry," said Ava.

"You're sick. Don't apologize."

Ava nodded slowly, her gaze dropped to the ground. "I am sick and I need my medicine. You don't know what it's like to be as sick as I am. I can't eat. I can't sleep. I can't do anything other than look for the next dose. In fact, there's nothing I won't do." Ava met Madelyn's gaze and looked away. "It's awful."

Madelyn paused. From Ava's point of view, the drugs were necessary. Yet in reality, they were the problem. "There are things that can be given to you to help with the pain and insomnia—other medications to fight the worst of your addiction."

Ava shook her head. "I've tried all those. They don't work. Maddie, I'm sorry, but I think I'm going to hell for everything that I've done."

"No! Just focus on getting better, that's all."

Ava's eyes flashed. Her jaw tightened. "You don't get it, do you? I don't want to get better."

"You don't? What do you want, then?"

"To tell you I'm sorry."

"For what?"

A door opened, creaking on its hinges. Madelyn turned to the sound. Her heart plummeted to her middle. Oleg Zavalov stood on the threshold of the presentation room. His face was a tapestry of injuries—bruises and scrapes. One eye was swollen shut and his bottom lip protruded.

Roman had beaten him.

She'd shot him.

He was swept away by the creek.

But he was here. Alive.

"She's sorry for leading you to me," Oleg said, answering the question for Ava.

"You're dead," Madelyn said.

He ran his hand through his hair and smiled. His lip split and the crack filled with bright red blood. "I was, but hell refused to take me. So, here I am."

Madelyn's throat closed, the inside of her chest burned—as if sliced open. Her face was hot and numb all at once. She knew the feeling. It was betrayal. In an instant, Madelyn was flung back to a memory from more than fifteen years ago. Madelyn had been ten, her sister twelve.

The day had been hot and hazy. It was late July. Too much summer had gone by to find pleasure in the endless days of nothing to do, and too much of it remained to mourn their passage. Ava and Madelyn, bored and hungry, had asked their mother to take them to the store for candy. Their mother had refused, but gave permission for them to walk together, provided they used their own money.

Neither sister had a penny to her name. But their father threw his spare change into a drawer of his desk. Who would notice if a handful of quarters went missing? Ava had asked.

Pockets loaded with money, Madelyn and Ava had bought everything from soda, to chips, to candy and gum. Upon their return, their mother was none the wiser. Madelyn and Ava congratulated themselves on their cunning and went about their day.

That night at dinner, with the incident almost swept clean from Madelyn's mind, Ava told their father that Madelyn had stolen his money to buy junk food. Ava swore that she'd told Madelyn not to. Ava knew that stealing was wrong and that Madelyn should not get away with being a thief.

Madelyn's memory ended there. She did not recall what her parents had said, nor the punishment meted out by her father. But she did remember the moment Ava spoke up, the cut and burn of betrayal.

And once again, Ava had lied and betrayed Madelyn. Only this time, it wasn't child's play.

"Ava." Madelyn turned to her sister. "How could you?" Her throat constricted. A million moments of sisterly love were shattered and Madelyn strangled on the last word until it was only a broken sound.

Before Ava could answer, Oleg rushed toward Madelyn.

Madelyn knew that there were three physiological reactions to danger. In the animal kingdom, it was all instinct. A cornered tiger became a fierce combatant; gazelles fled. And a rabbit, sensing a hawk in the sky, held itself in statue-like stillness, in hopes that it would be overlooked.

But in humans it was as much upbringing, conditioning and society as it was brain chemistry. Which meant that in many ways, people chose their reactions to fear and threats: fight, flight or freeze.

It was the last instinct which first gripped Madelyn. Then Roman's face flashed into her mind, along with the training he had given her. She made the choice to fight—to win—to live.

Oleg smiled again, the bloody lip now oozing. He swung out. Madelyn ducked, but his fist slammed into the side of her head. A burst of pain exploded in her skull and then swept downward until her jaw ached.

She dove forward. Grabbing Oleg by the ankles, she pulled up and shouldered his knees back. The man fell over. Madelyn, on hands and knees, clambered toward the door. Oleg grabbed her foot, pulling her back.

She breathed deeply, smoothing away the sharpest edges of panic that filled her chest. Like Roman had instructed, Madelyn marshaled her strength. She focused it in her heel and aimed for a place six inches behind Oleg's eye. She kicked out, her foot connecting. Oleg roared in pain. Rearing back, he let her go.

On her feet, Madelyn reached the door and gripped the handle. She jerked the door open, then stopped. She'd gotten away, but what about Ava? If Madelyn left now, her sister would soon be dead—either by Oleg's hand or the abuse she inflicted on her own body.

Madelyn was done being the rabbit, or even the gazelle. She was the tiger, and even if Oleg Zavalov had her by the tail right now, she'd force him to let go and then introduce him to her claws. She turned, her arm swinging in a wide arc. She caught Oleg in the side of the head and her fist throbbed. He stumbled back, shaking his head like a wet dog.

She waited for him to advance. Bracing her back on the door, Madelyn kicked out and caught him in the middle. He doubled over and retched. Cursing her name, he wiped his mouth.

The nose. The eyes. The throat. All the pressure points that Roman had shared came back to her.

She reached for the back of his head and drove her knee into his face. Bone connected with bone. Madelyn's leg throbbed, but Oleg toppled backward and sprawled across the floor. He didn't get up. Ava was still in the chair, catatonic, and Madelyn limped to her sister. She had to get them both out of there, but how?

"Ava?" Madelyn pulled on her sister's arm, trying to bring her to standing. Ava remained limp in the chair. Madelyn knelt and slipped her arm under her sister's shoulder. She tried to stand, but Ava—though skeletal—was also deadweight, and she didn't make it completely to her feet. A noise caught her attention but before Madelyn could turn, agony ricocheted through her skull.

Then there was nothing.

Roman used back roads to get from Denver's airport to Boulder, pulling into Madelyn's parking space in record time. Pausing, he put the gearshift into Park and wondered how she might react to his return. Then again, he didn't have the luxury of worry. If his instincts were correct, then Oleg Zavalov was alive, mobile and a danger to Madelyn.

Taking the stairs two at a time, he knocked on her door with force. "Madelyn," he said to the doorjamb. "It's Roman. There've been some developments. We need to talk."

He waited for an answer. None came. He knocked again, using the side of his fist. The door shook in its frame. "Madelyn. It's Roman."

He tried the handle and it held fast. He knocked again. No answer. Slipping his wallet from the back pocket of his pants, Roman withdrew a credit card. After picking the lock, he opened the door.

"Madelyn? It's Roman. Sorry that I opened your door. I have news."

She wasn't home, he could tell that as he stepped inside. It was as if her absence made the apartment duller or turned the air stale. He closed the door and examined his surroundings. A single table lamp illuminated the room. A towel, draped over the back of a kitchen chair, was still damp. Madelyn's laptop sat open on the coffee table. Beyond those three minor details, the room was just as it had been when Roman left.

He wandered to her bedroom. The clothes she had been wearing lay in a pile by the bathroom door and the fruity floral scent of shampoo hung in the air. Roman returned to the main living space. No books were scattered across the floor, nor were any broken dishes strewn about—nothing to make Roman think there had been a struggle, or that Madelyn had left under duress.

If she wasn't here, the question became—where had she gone? And was it his business to find out? There were several possibilities, groceries, class, hospital rounds, tearfully replaying the past twenty-four hours to a *friend*. Maybe an email or text would provide a clue to where she'd gone. He sat on the sofa and reached for her laptop. If her errand was innocuous, he told himself, he'd put her computer back and wait in the car for her return.

The computer was password protected, but no match for Roman's technical expertise. He did a hard shutdown, before rebooting with lines of code that circumvented her security. Madelyn would be unhappy, to put it mildly, with Roman looking at her computer without permission. But what if there was a threat? He wouldn't be doing his job if he didn't try to find her.

The screen came to life and Roman went directly to the most likely place for communication—her texts. Out of more than a dozen conversations, there was only one to which she'd replied. It was with her sister, Ava.

Ava: I need help. Come and get me.

Another text followed with a Boulder address.

Sent 5:04 a.m.

Ava: Maddie.

Sent 5:05 a.m.

Ava: Are you there?
Sent 5:05 a.m.
Ava: Why are you ignoring me?
Sent: 5:05 a.m.
Read 5:56 p.m.
Madelyn: I'm here. Anything you need.
Madelyn: Ava?
Sent 5:56 p.m.
Delivered 5:56 p.m.
Read 5:56 p.m.
Ava: I'm here.
Sent 6:02 p.m.
Read 6:02 p.m.
Madelyn: Do you still want to meet? Are you
at the same place?
Sent 6:03 p.m.
Read 6:03 p.m.
Ava: Yes meet. Diffr't plc.
Sent 6:03 p.m.
Read 6:03 p.m.
Madelyn: Where?
Sent 6:03 p.m.
Read: 6:03 p.m.
Ava: Are you alone.
Sent 6:04 p.m.
Read 6:04 p.m.
Madelyn: Yes. Why?
Sent 6:04 p.m.
Read 6:04 p.m.
Ava: Meet me at University Memorial Center.

2nd floor study lounge. 6:30.
Sent 6:04 p.m.
Read 6:04 p.m.
Madelyn: OMW
On my way.

There were roughly a million things Roman didn't like about this scenario. The first, and most obvious, was that there had been contact at all. Ava had been in Boulder for months, Roman knew that fact firsthand. She hadn't contacted her sister in all that time and then the same day that Madelyn runs awry of Oleg, Ava needed help?

And yet, how would Oleg make the connection? Unless you knew the two to be sisters, the resemblance wasn't noticeable. Then again, someone— presumably Oleg—had been in Madelyn's apartment and taken great interest in a photo of Ava and Madelyn. For someone with as many street connections as Oleg, finding Ava wouldn't be hard. But could he get one sister to betray the other?

The location was also off. The University of Colorado's student union was not a place Ava would know well. But someone like Oleg might. His men sold drugs on the campus regularly.

Before he added any more oddities to his list, Roman was on his feet and out the door. He slid into the driver's seat and started the engine. Tires screeching, he used the car's phone system to call Ian.

As soon as the ringing ceased, Roman began to

speak. "Oleg's not dead," he said. "Somehow or another, Zavalov survived. Her sister contacted her and wanted to meet. I think it's a set-up."

"An interesting theory," said Ian, "but doubtful."

Doubtful? Roman wanted to bellow. "What do you mean?"

"You're assuming a lot."

"That's part of my job, to take information and make an analysis. I hate to break it to you, but all analysis is based on assumptions." Along with gut feelings—and Roman's stomach was sick with the possibilities.

"True," said Ian, "but we just got word from the Colorado Bureau of Investigation's search and rescue team. Oleg Zavalov's jacket was found tangled in some debris about five miles downstream from where the bridge washed out. There's a bullet hole through the chest. The shot would've been fatal."

"Are you sure the jacket's his?"

"His name is embroidered on the inside pocket."

Roman cursed. "I'm telling you, he's out there."

"And I'm telling you, he's not. Oleg Zavalov is dead. It's only a matter of time before his body is found. What we do have is a new lead on Nikolai Mateev. The Transportation Safety Administration just came in with a report. Photo recognition has a 78 percent match for Mateev on a flight landing in Colorado Springs within the hour. I'm on my way now. Are you coming?"

Roman exhaled and considered his options. A bullet to the chest was a hard wound to survive under the best circumstances and Oleg's situation had been far from optimal. Maybe Oleg's car had simply been stolen. The timing of Ava's contact might also be co-incidental. If that was the case, then he'd have a long list of petty crimes against a woman he was trying to protect—breaking and entering, hacking into her computer, stalking.

Madelyn wouldn't be flattered.

If he turned south now, he could meet Ian in Colorado Springs and be there to arrest Nikolai Mateev. The point of the spear, gleaming in the sunlight, beckoned to Roman.

But what if he wasn't wrong? Until he saw Oleg's dead body on a slab in the mortuary, there was a possibility that he was out there. What if Ava had been used to lure Madelyn into a deadly trap and Roman ignored his hunch?

Amid the rush hour traffic, Roman saw the sign for I-25 South, the road to Denver and then Colorado Springs beyond. It was the same intersection that led, when taken to the left, to CU's main campus. The light turned red and Roman pulled to a stop.

"Are you there?" Ian asked. "Are you coming? Can we count on you to see this Mateev business to the end?"

Madelyn. Nikolai. Oleg. Roman wanted to be in three places at once.

Yet, as he stared at the traffic light, he knew there was only one decision to make. Flipping on his blinker, he gave Ian his answer. When the light changed from red to green, Roman stepped down on the gas and rocketed toward the one thing that mattered most.

Madelyn.

Madelyn knew she was injured before her eyes opened. Her head hurt and her tongue was thick, her eyes gritty. She was lying on her stomach, her face to the ground. Short, rough carpet imprinted on her cheeks. A damp and musty smell was overwhelming and she gagged. Cold from the floor seeped through her clothes. All these facts she knew as absolutes as well as her name and her enrollment in CU's medical school. What she didn't know was where she was or what had happened prior to this moment.

She searched her memory for a specific instance to gauge the passage of time, like a thumbtack on a map. Threads of memories came to her, but nothing substantial to which she could cling and begin to weave a cloth that made up the past few hours. Or maybe it had been days.

Not knowing where she was—or when—was a common side effect of head trauma. Of that fact, she was certain. She recalled counseling the mother of a middle school football player with a concussion that her son might lose two or three days leading up to the injury. At the time—she didn't know when— Madelyn had said that it was common and that something could trigger the boy's memories.

Madelyn allowed her eyelids to flutter open and saw only the seam between the gray carpeted floor and a cinder block wall of the same color. Had she fallen? She tried to picture herself upon a ladder and then losing her balance. The image came to her, but held no truth.

She rolled to her side and pushed up to her elbow. Pain shot through her skull and a wave of nausea swelled. She breathed deeply and the queasiness ebbed. The pain remained, though, becoming a throbbing ache at the back of her head that mirrored her heartbeat.

From behind, came the scuffing sound of shoe leather on the carpeted floor. She turned. The movement released a rushing tide inside her head. Blood filled her ears and light flashed through her field of vision. Madelyn sucked in a deep breath and waited for the symptoms to abate.

An attractive man with slicked-back dark hair knelt next to Madelyn. He looked as if he'd been in a car wreck. Bruises and scrapes covered his face. Maybe the car crash was where she'd been hurt, as well. In her mind's eye Madelyn saw a black luxury sedan on a dirt road. The image was like quicksilver, gone as soon as she tightened her grasp. It left her with nothing and wondering what she had held in the first place.

The man moved closer. His eyes were as black as coal and she was positive that she'd looked into them before. She tried not to shiver. "Who are you?" she asked.

"You don't remember me?"

Madelyn's mouth went dry. "Not at all."

"Are you kidding me?"

"No. I wish I could remember…" The tingling sensation of panic danced at the base of her spine. "But, I can't."

"I'm Oleg. Oleg Zavalov."

"Oleg Zavalov." Madelyn let the words roll around in her mouth. "Your name sounds familiar."

But from where? For some reason, she didn't think that she liked him—never mind that he'd left her on the cold floor. Or maybe she'd just fallen and he was waiting for paramedics to arrive.

Oleg sat back on his heels. In the toes of his expensive shoes reflected the overhead light. The glare cut through her scalp and intensified her pain. He whistled low. "I'll be damned. You don't recall a thing, do you?"

Irritation overrode her confusion and she snapped. "You think I like not being able to remember the last day or two?"

"Calm down," he said as he held up his hands. His palms soft and white. Madelyn immediately decided that Oleg was like his shoes, too polished to be anything beyond show.

She must've recently met Oleg. But where? It brought up an interesting question, though—who was he to her? She couldn't imagine herself interested in Oleg romantically. He was nothing like the last guy she dated. What was his name?

In a flash, she saw a man with hazel eyes and a day's growth of beard. He stood by a window and looked out at the mountains. She caught a whiff of pine and rain. Without question, she knew that she had loved the other man, might love him still. Yet could bring up nothing more about him.

"Did you call the ambulance?" Madelyn asked.

"What?"

"I assume that I fell," she said. She cast her gaze around the room, looking for the ladder from which she had toppled, and found none. She was in a windowless office. The carpeting was the cheap industrial kind and there was a desk with a chair, a set of filing cabinets and another metal chair in the middle of the room. Overhead, strips of florescent light hummed.

"Yeah, that's it," said Oleg. "You slipped. I called the ambulance and they'll be here any minute." He stood and held out his hand to her. "You want to sit in the chair? It's better than the floor. Come on, I'll help you up."

Madelyn placed her hand in his. Oleg's flesh was cold, damp, and she wanted to recoil at his touch. Instead, she allowed him to pull her to her feet. Her equilibrium was off and she listed to the side. Oleg placed his arm around her shoulder, helping her to stay upright. Though he had been nothing beyond courteous, something was wrong. But what? She couldn't concentrate—not through the pain and nausea and the lights that danced in her vision.

Arm still on her shoulder, Oleg led Madelyn to the chair. Her legs gave out and she practically fell into the seat. Madelyn was exhausted and she longed to lie down and sleep. Somehow, her brain remembered that slumber was the worst idea with a head injury.

"Can I see your hand?" Oleg asked.

She hesitated and glanced at her palms. They looked normal and nothing hurt. "They're fine," she said.

"Your hand," he said again. "Let me see it."

Even in her confused state, Madelyn found his question odd. Yet she had no reason to argue. "Sure." She held up her palm.

Oleg grabbed her and wrenched her hand hard behind her back. A band encircled her wrist. The stiff plastic tightened and bit into her flesh. She flailed and tried to stand to run. Oleg kicked her in the chest, driving all the air from her lungs and slamming her into the chair. He straddled her, pinning her down. He grabbed her other hand and soon it was cuffed behind her, as well.

"Madelyn." Oleg moved to stand before her. He sounded so calm, she couldn't help but focus on his face. A lock of his hair fell over his forehead. He smoothed it back into place. "Are you sure you don't remember me?"

"I'm positive. I don't know anything."

"If you're telling me the truth, then more's the pity."

Her pulse raced, sending white flashes spiraling through her vision. Madelyn jerked her arms. They were held tight to the legs of the chair. She pushed up to stand. The chair remained steady.

"Your seat is bolted to the floor," Oleg offered. "You aren't going anywhere."

If she couldn't escape, then she needed to have him see her as a person. "Why is it a pity if I can't remember you?" she asked.

"Because your suffering will be much worse if you don't remember your sins."

Oleg drew back his fist and hit Madelyn in the face. Her mouth throbbed and filled with blood. Her heart seized as her veins filled with icy terror. He hit her again and again, relentless. She no longer had time to feel fear, only pain that exploded like fireworks each time he struck her.

Oleg stopped and stepped away from Madelyn. His knuckles were bruised. He cupped his injured hand with the other. "I'm going to ask you this once," he said. "Where's Roman?"

"I don't know anyone named Roman," Madelyn said.

"Bull. You do."

Oleg struck her with the back of his hand. Her head snapped as her eyes filled with tears. She was desperate to make the beating stop. What did he want? Some guy she'd never even heard of? What did it hurt her to tell Oleg what he wanted to hear? "He's gone," she said quickly, before he had a chance to strike her again. "He left town. He's afraid of someone, it might be you. But that memory's fuzzy, too."

"That's exactly what I thought," Oleg said. He shook out his hand. "Well, then, you will have plenty of time to beg for forgiveness for the both of you."

Madelyn tensed, bracing for another blow. It didn't come. Oleg walked away from her. He turned off the light and closed the door, entombing Madelyn in the darkness and the silence.

Chapter 10

Tires screeching, Roman rounded the corner. The entrance to CU's campus lay directly ahead. A traffic light hung above the intersection and changed from green to yellow. He accelerated, crossing the road just as it turned to red. He barreled past the information booth and skirted the outside of campus, recalling the news reports of the planned protests by the student body.

He pulled into a parking place in front of the student union and turned off the ignition. Roman was through the front doors and on the second floor before the engine quieted. He slid a gun into the small of his back, letting his waistband hold it in place and his shirttail hide it.

It took him less than a minute to find a room marked as Second Floor Study Lounge. It was an out-of-the-way place on a regular day, and today the Memorial Union was all but abandoned. He opened the door and crossed the threshold. A motion light turned on, illuminating the room. A woman sat in a chair, asleep. Roman recognized her at once.

"Ava," he said from the doorway.

She didn't move.

He tried again, halfway across the room and louder this time. "Ava."

Still nothing.

He moved to the chair and kicked the edge. "Ava."

Her eyelids rolled open. "Go away. I'm sleeping. I've been sick." She closed her eyes.

"Ava," he repeated, undeterred by her claim at illness and obvious use of drugs. "Ava, I need to find your sister, Madelyn."

Without opening her eyes, Ava licked her lips and sighed. "Everyone wants Maddie and nobody cares about Ava. Maddie goes to college and then medical school, all Ava does is get high and disappoint everyone."

Roman's heart raced. "Who else wants Madelyn?"

Ava's head lolled to the side. He kicked the edge of the chair again. "Ava."

Nothing.

Roman reached for his phone and brought up Ian's contact. He paused, and put the phone back.

A full-fledge raid on The Prow, the most likely

place that Madelyn was taken, would meet considerable reluctance. Nikolai Mateev was too big a prize to redirect their much-needed resources. Besides, the powers that be assumed Oleg was dead.

No matter how much he needed to see justice served for both Nikolai Mateev and Oleg Zavalov, Madelyn's life was the most important thing to him. And in order to save her, Roman would do anything.

Including breaking all the rules.

He left the room and sped down the corridor. Rounding a corner, Roman ran into a man wearing the dark blue uniform of a Boulder police officer. The other man's face went pale.

"Jackson," Roman snarled. He grabbed the cop by the neck and shoved him up against the wall. "This is no coincidence that you're here right now. You've heard from Oleg, and don't deny it." Roman took Jackson's own firearm and tucked it into the small of his back.

Jackson held up his hands in surrender. Gone was the cocky police officer on the take. "What do you want me to say? You're right. He called and told me I had to help him. He threatened to turn over evidence to my superiors if I didn't. Sure, I hung out at The Prow and I drank for free. My presence gave him some bona fides. I ignored a few things, but never broke the law. Not until now..."

"Give me a reason I shouldn't break your neck."

"I came back to check on Ava. I know her from the bar. They're all lost souls if they start hanging around The Prow. She was different, I don't know. But she didn't look good when I was here before and I thought I should call the EMTs."

"Came back?" Roman tightened his grip on the other man's throat. Jackson's eyes bugged out and his face turned red. "Where had you gone? Never mind, I know. Oleg enlisted your help dealing with Madelyn. Tell me this—" Roman swallowed "—is she alive?"

"She was, but she was hurt—unconscious. I'm not sure what he did to her before, or what he plans to do with her now."

"Why did he bring you in?"

"Oleg needed this building cleared out and a guard while he got Madelyn in his car."

"Where are they now?"

"I told you, I'm not sure."

"If you're lying…" Roman clenched his fist.

"I'm not," Jackson choked. "I'm sorry…"

Roman wasn't in the mood for apologies, he wanted retribution. Then again, he needed help and Jackson might be the only person he could count on right now. If Jackson called in Ava's condition as an overdose, she'd be treated, sent to the county jail for a night and then let back out on the streets by morning. By tomorrow, she'd once again be on the unending hamster wheel of addiction and most likely—on the run.

That wasn't what Madelyn would want for her sister. It wasn't what he wanted, either.

"Can you hold Ava as a material witness?"

"For what?" Jackson asked.

"As an accessory to kidnapping," Roman said. "Ava texted Madelyn and asked that she come and meet her here. Certainly, those texts were sent at Oleg's behest."

"I guess so."

Roman released his hold on Jackson's neck. The other man crumpled to the ground. On hands and knees, the cop slobbered and wheezed. Roman knelt before him. "Take care of Ava," he said, "and if you are truly sorry, get some of your fellow police officers—the honest kind—to The Prow. I'm going to need backup."

Oleg pulled into the parking lot adjacent to the downtown bus terminal and mentally repeated the lie that he needed Nikolai Mateev to believe. He opened the glove box for the umpteenth time to make certain he'd brought the bug Roman Black planted in his office. A new bus pulled up and Oleg watched as the passengers shuffled down the stairs and ambled toward the terminal.

One of the last people to disembark, Nikolai was a large man in both height and girth. With sparse white hair, he wore khaki pants, a white polo shirt and a polar fleece jacket of navy blue. He carried a single duffel bag, emblazoned with a Colorado Mustangs logo. There was nothing in his appearance that spoke of money, power or influence. In fact, Nikolai Mateev looked average and boring. Oleg couldn't help but sag at his first impression, deflated with disappointment.

Despite appearances, Nikolai truly was rich and influential. He had the ability to give Oleg the life he'd always wanted. If only Oleg could explain away his recent foibles, that was.

Opening the door, Oleg stood next to his car and waved. Nikolai nodded and ambled slowly toward him. *"Privet, Otets,"* Oleg said as Nikolai approached. *Hello, Father.*

Nikolai ignored the greeting and slid into the passenger seat, closing the door with a slam. "I am in America now and will speak English to fit in," Nikolai said. "You will only speak English to me, *ponimayu*?" *Understand?*

"Are we waiting for more people?" Oleg asked. He assumed that a man with almost mythical status would travel with an entourage—even on a Greyhound bus.

"No more people," he said. "We travel separately and will rendezvous in Denver." Nikolai then went on to explain that seven different groups had come into the country via distinctive routes. It was meant to keep American law enforcement off balance and always running—if they ever got word of his arrival, that was.

Oleg had to agree, the plan was wholly unexpected and, therefore, brilliant. He nodded his approval.

"I thought Serge would be here to greet me," Nikolai said. "What is he doing that is so important?"

That was the one question Oleg wanted to avoid answering and he was eager to change the subject. Yet, what would he gain by putting off the inevitable? He took in a deep breath and grimaced at the residual pain from being shot. "There have been some developments," Oleg said. "Unfortunate developments."

"Da?"

For a moment, Oleg lost his confidence. His stomach dropped to his bowels and his hands trembled. He gave a fleeting thought to telling Nikolai the truth. Yet Oleg had lied to the godfather of the Russian mob when he said that Serge was fine earlier in the day. Any subsequent story must fit that narrative. To Oleg's own defense, he'd been caught off guard and had spoken without thought. That had been his mistake and one he wouldn't repeat. He stuck to his prepared comments. "It seems as if Serge was after your money…"

"It is his money, too. I named him my heir. He can have anything he wants…"

The hairs on the back of Oleg's neck stood on end. He hadn't expected that response. "He wanted your position, your power, your empire. I found an electronic listening device in my office and evidence that they were trying to find all the accounts. I confronted them and they shot me and tried to drown me."

"Vran'ye!" Lies! Nikolai snarled.

Oleg turned to him. "Look at my face. My injuries. Do they lie?"

Nikolai glared and huffed a breath.

"And this?" Oleg opened the glove box and handed over the bug. "This is the ELD I found."

Nikolai examined the black plastic box from all sides. "It is highly advanced, no?"

"It is. They convinced an employee of mine to betray me—betray you. He's dead, but his girlfriend is at my bar. She helped as well, and is now eager to corroborate my story." Oleg had no idea what Madelyn would say at first, but like he had long known—a person being tortured will say anything to make the pain stop. And in the end, that's all that mattered.

"Serge?" Oleg asked.

"I'm sorry to say, but he's dead. Anton killed him and then I shot Anton." To Oleg's thinking, it was better to not have had a hand in Serge's death.

Nikolai looked out the window and mumbled, "I never liked Anton."

"Are you hungry?" Oleg asked. "We can stop and get you something to eat."

"I have no appetite. I am sick and tired." He closed his eyes and pinched the bridge of his nose. The older man had transformed from robust into gray and drawn in just minutes.

"Sick?" Oleg asked.

"That is a, what do you call it? It's an American phrase, no? The trip on the bus was thirty-six hours, all to learn that my great-nephew betrayed me. He's not actually blood of my blood—only related to me by my wife. Greatness is in the blood you know. I am glad that you are with me, Oleg Zavalov. You are a good man, from an old and respected family. I knew your grandmother and she prepared you well. I will make sure that you go far. And maybe we do have time for a meal."

Oleg's heart began to beat in a strong and steady rhythm. It was the footfalls of his ancestors as generations of Zavalovs trod through the Kremlin, Saint Basil's Cathedral and the Winter Palace in Saint Petersburg. Important men doing the business of those who reigned supreme, and now Oleg could count himself among their ranks.

Roman circled the block, searching both sides of the street for Oleg Zavalov's car. It was nowhere to be seen. Where the hell was Oleg and—more important—where was Madelyn? Roman took a third pass. Nothing. What if he had been wrong? What if Oleg hadn't brought Madelyn back to The Prow? She could be anywhere by now and Roman didn't have a clue as to where he should look.

Ahead, The Prow's automatic neon lights came on, spilling onto the broken sidewalk, calling to Roman and challenging him to investigate his folly. He threw the car into Park and stepped onto the street, tucking Jackson's purloined firearm into the small of his back.

He scanned the street once more and saw nothing. Anger, like lava from the pit of the earth, filled him and propelled him forward. He never should have left Madelyn alone. He'd been disappointed and embarrassed when she'd turned him away, and then too proud to insist that he needed to stay.

And now she was gone.

A handwritten sign hung on The Prow's door. Four words in Oleg's scrawl said it all: Closed Until Further Notice. Roman tried the handle, it was locked. He hadn't expected anything less, although it didn't matter. Within a minute, he had picked the lock. Slowly, quietly, Roman pushed the door open and reengaged the lock. He entered the darkened bar and listened. There was no sound beyond the rush of his pulse as it resonated within his chest.

He crossed the room and stopped at the basement door. He pushed on the metal bar that controlled the lock. It depressed and the door swung open. It was strange that the door had been left unlocked, unless there was nothing else in the basement for Oleg to hide. Roman squinted into the gloom. The first two stairs were visible and beyond that—blackness.

As he stood at the door, his pulse racing, it came back to him.

If hell was cold and dark, then the cave in Afghanistan was the entrance. The memories of that day were almost as real as the one he was living. The mission was simple: extract the soldiers, kill the bad guys. Just like a surgery to remove a cancer, and Roman was the scalpel's edge. He'd snuck into the cave—silent and vigilant. The rest of his team followed. The first combatant he found was a guard. His life was ended with a knife to the throat before he had a chance to sound the alarm. Four more men fell, their hot blood awash on Roman's hands.

The combatants must have felt their location deep in the Hindu Kush was remote enough to evade detection because there were no other guards beyond the initial five. Less than a quarter of a klick into the cave, there was an antechamber. That's where Roman found the US soldiers. The men were bound, blindfolded and gagged—all of them, just sitting against that wall. It looked like they'd been there for days. The smell was worse than any latrine Roman ever had the misfortune to run across.

Light from a nearby room leaked in, along with voices. Roman knew enough Pashto to piece together what the terrorists were saying. They were trying to uplink with a satellite so that the soldiers' execution could be broadcast over the internet in real time.

One by one, the men from Delta Force helped the soldiers to their feet and ushered them out of the cave. Had everything gone perfectly, they all would have slipped into the night, and an incoming Hellfire missile would have said farewell for them. Of course, nothing ever went as planned. There was an American soldier with a broken leg. Roman was the intel officer who should have known about the injury. The other man could barely stand, much less walk. His first step faltered. The sound was slight, but alerted the enemy nonetheless.

Bullets. Light. Noise. Pain.

Roman grimaced as fire filled his foot. It was a

fair payment for missing the other man's injury. As the cave vanished from his memory, Roman realized that it wasn't just his foot that had been injured on that mission.

His hope for a better future had been destroyed when the army let him go. Sure, he was injured—but did that mean he couldn't serve? Or was his mistake also his career's undoing? There it was; the fear that lurked just beneath the surface.

It was because of Madelyn that he could finally look his personal demons in the face, and see beyond them to a brighter day.

Focused on the here and now, Roman listened again for movement and heard nothing, not even his breath this time. Roman had never given up before, but he knew there were major flaws in his analysis.

Yet, if Oleg hadn't brought Madelyn to The Prow, Roman didn't have enough intel to look elsewhere. For the first time in his life, Roman cared enough to be afraid.

Madelyn's faculties returned. She still didn't know where she was or what she supposedly had done, but her thinking was clear and she had assessed her situation—to a degree.

The most important fact she discovered was that flexi cuffs had been used to tie her to the chair. Another fact: a bolt stuck out near her right hand. If she lifted her shoulder and listed to the side, she made contact with the serrated edge. Madelyn pulled the plastic cuff back and forth, back and forth, slowly sawing through the plastic. As she worked, her mood swung wildly between hope for survival and becoming morose over the futility of her situation. More often, pessimism won out. Even if she freed one hand, she would still be stuck to the chair. The door would remain out of reach, and locked.

And yet, Madelyn knew she wasn't the type of person to sit idly.

That connection with her true self gave Madelyn courage. The plastic dug into her skin and the metal bolt ripped her flesh. She ignored the pain and redoubled her effort. Sweat covered her skin, collecting at her brow and trailing down her face.

The plastic broke. Pain surged through Madelyn's arm. It ended with pinpricks dancing along her palm as blood returned to the extremity. She shook her hand to relieve more of the discomfort.

The sounds of the door handle moving came from just outside the room. It meant only one thing—the door would soon be open. She was still bound, but a flash of memory came to her. A male voice gave her instructions, *A surprise attack is always best, but strike hard and fast. Nose. Throat. Eyes. Aim six inches beyond where you want to hit.*

Could she give herself the edge by launching a surprise attack? Madelyn sat back in her chair, her chin on her chest, and feigned unconsciousness. The door swung open. The overhead light came on and registered as yellow and red flashes beyond her closed eyes.

"Madelyn." Her name drifted across the room on a whisper. "Madelyn? Can you hear me?"

She recognized the voice and fought to not react. It came from the same person who'd given her the lessons on self-defense. The man's face appeared in her mind. This time his hands were on her breasts, lying beneath her, in the middle of making love. She had cared for him then. Did she care for him now? He was involved in this whole deadly game, that she unquestionably knew. What she didn't know, was if he could be trusted or not.

She sensed him kneeling before her. His fingertips grazed her cheek. "Madelyn," he said again.

She couldn't pretend to be comatose any longer and her lids drifted open. She looked into his deep green eyes and every event of the last twenty-four hours came back to her in a rush. The photo of Ava. The kiss in the basement. The accusations and threats. Their escape from Boulder, followed by the time at the cabin. Every memory returned with her next breath.

"Roman," she said, his name making her whole.

Oleg popped another French fry in his mouth and shook his cup so that the last of his milkshake settled at the bottom. He usually treated his body as a temple, and on any other day would never defile the sacred space with fast food. But Nikolai insisted they go through an American drive-through. Oleg—his newest emissary—happily acquiesced.

The restaurant hadn't been far from The Prow, and Oleg hadn't been gone long. Still, as he approached, he remained vigilant for any unusual activity on the street. There was none. Oleg smothered a greasy belch, confident that Madelyn was still in the basement, still cuffed to the chair and still ready to tell him what he wanted her to say. He sipped noisily through a straw and pulled up to the curb.

Nikolai Mateev wiped his lips with a paper napkin. "We have fast food in Moscow, you know. But even in America, the burgers are better."

Oleg gestured to The Prow. "Once inside, I'll get you an American beer to wash down your dinner."

"I usually drink vodka, but as an American, I'll drink your beer." He chuckled.

Oleg laughed with him, yet found the conversation as dull and banal as Nikolai had looked when he trudged from the bus. But there was more to Mateev. There had to be. And until he revealed his true self, Oleg had no choice but to wait.

Oleg got out of the car and checked the street again. He found nothing amiss and rounded to open Nikolai's door. As they approached the bar, Oleg's stomach churned and he knew that later he'd regret having eaten all that rot to keep Nikolai happy.

Just as Oleg had left it, the front door was locked and a handwritten note about the bar being closed was still in place. After producing the keys, Oleg unlocked the door and held it open for Nikolai. Oleg stepped across the threshold into the darkened bar. It was a step Oleg had taken tens of thousands of times before. Yet this time was different. In helping Nikolai Mateev, Oleg had done what his grandmother always foretold—become an important man. He could almost hear the cheer of the crowds that filled Red Square, even though the adulation came from centuries long past.

Roman knelt in front of Madelyn and let out a long breath, a sense of profound relief washing over him. One arm was loose and the other attached to the chair by a flexi cuff. But she was alive and that was all that mattered right now.

"How'd you find me?" she asked.

"One part good analysis, two parts dumb luck." He wanted to pull Madelyn to him and let his body melt into her perfect form. He had to resist the urge to be anything other than vigilant. Still, he needed to be honest with her. "I hope you aren't mad, I went back to your apartment and when you weren't there, I let myself in. I was worried that Oleg was alive and mobile, so I read the texts on your computer..."

"It was Ava," Madelyn said. "She set me up."

Tears filled her eyes and she worked her jaw back and forth. It was a bad betrayal and one that would haunt Madelyn for years to come. To give her comfort, he reached for her free hand. Her palm was sticky and covered in blood. Flesh had been sheared away, leaving exposed pink skin that filled with pin-pricks of blood. The side of her wrist had gotten the worst of it, crimson blood freely ran from an open gash. Roman gripped her arm hard and lifted the extremity—both simple first aid measures to staunch the bleeding.

"There's an exposed bolt under the seat," she said, giving him an explanation of how her wrist had been injured before he had the chance to ask. "I used it to cut the flexi cuff and ended up ripping more than just plastic. Oleg tied me to this chair to beat me." She shivered. Roman continued to hold her and gave Madelyn a moment to collect her thoughts. "It was awful and I was terrified."

"Where is he now?"

"I don't know."

"Did he say when he was coming back?"

Madelyn shook her head. "No. I was so worried that he was just going to leave me here to waste away."

It was an interesting notion. Yet, Oleg had gone to an extreme amount of trouble to kidnap Madelyn. It meant that Oleg needed her for something? But what?

"He's coming back," Roman said. "It's the only thing that makes any sense."

Madelyn jerked her tethered arm as she tried to stand and run. The chair, bolted to the floor, rocked and then jerked her back to her seat. "Get me out of here," she said, on the verge of sheer panic.

"Madelyn." He gripped her knees. "It won't do either one of us any good if you panic. I want you to breathe with me."

She began to breathe slowly, deeply, along with him. Her struggles ceased.

"Are you better?"

"I am but..." She cast her gaze to the side. "Did you see Ava?"

He nodded. "At the university. She was high, but lucid enough to tell me she'd seen you. After that, I knew Oleg was involved. It's how I found you."

"Where is she now?"

"I grabbed a police officer and he's holding her as a material witness." Roman chose not to tell Madelyn that the cop was Jackson. "It'll get Ava into the system and hopefully the help she needs." He paused. "I hope that's what you wanted."

She nodded. "It is." Both her movement and voice were small.

"But I'm worried about you," Roman said. "Any other injuries?"

"Oleg knocked me out. It left my memory foggy for a little while, but I saw you and it all came back."

The importance of his face being the key to unlocking her memories did not escape Roman. He placed a gentle kiss on Madelyn's lips. "I need to find something to cut you lose," he said. He riffled through the desk drawers looking for scissors, a knife—hell, he'd even be happy with a letter opener. Nothing. "I'll be right back."

"I'm not going anywhere," she said.

Roman gave her a wry smile. He loved her spirit and her sense of humor. He loved her strength and compassion. Basically, he loved her. Too bad the feeling wasn't returned. With a final glance over his shoulder, he slipped across the hall and into the storage room.

It was just as Roman remembered—shelves filled with chips, salsa, cheap wine, popcorn. He rummaged through the foodstuffs for something sharp and was rewarded with a utility knife. The blade had been dulled by weeks of cutting boxes open, but was still sharp enough to slice through the remaining flexi cuff.

A noise came from above and Roman froze. The ceiling creaked, as if the floor overhead was giving way to a footstep. Then again and again. Someone was moving upstairs, of that Roman had no doubt. Which made the answer to the next question so important—was it Oleg? Or had Jackson found his ethics and brought in the cops?

He silently returned to Madelyn and cut the plastic band encircling her wrist. She rose to her feet and faltered. Roman held her steady. As if his hands needed proof that she was real, he ran his palms down her arms and encircled her waist.

She looked up at him, the harsh overhead light shone down on her like a halo. He drew her to him. She felt so good—soft and strong—but he wanted more, needed more.

Pulling Madelyn closer, Roman pressed his lips to hers. She sighed into his kiss and he slipped his tongue into her mouth. She reached around his neck, her body fitting perfectly with his form. For a moment, he almost forgot about the intruder upstairs. Almost, but not completely.

He broke away from the kiss, determined to make two things happen. First, he had to get Madelyn out of the building. Second, if Oleg was upstairs, there was no way that Roman was going to let him escape again.

"Come on," Roman said. He slipped his hand through Madelyn's. "Let's get you out of here."

"Me? Why not us?"

He didn't have a lot of time to explain, so he gave her the basics. "There are people upstairs. I don't know if it's Oleg or the police. I'm going to investigate, but first I want you to get out through the back door. The code is six-one-one-two."

"You aren't leaving me," she said, clinging to his arm. "I won't let you."

Her brows were drawn together in a look of determination. The injuries to her face pained his own flesh and the need to guard her was as essential as his next breath. "I can't do what I need to without knowing that you're safe."

"If I'm with you, how can I be anything but?" Before Roman could argue that there were several ways, she continued, "Oleg Zavalov has been chasing me for the past twenty-four hours. He's used my sister to trap me. I'm not going to keep running. If I do, I'll never stop looking over my shoulder."

In a way, she made sense. He handed Madelyn the utility knife and he reached for his gun. "If I tell you to run, you have to do as I say. Got it?"

She tucked the packing knife into her back pocket. "Got it."

Light from the office spilled into the hallway and chased darkness into the farthest corners of the corridor. It illuminated the bottom of the stairs and slowly the glow faded to nothing until the uppermost steps were lost in the gloom. Hand in hand, Roman and Madelyn ascended.

At the top, Roman held his ear to the door and heard two distinct voices in the room beyond, both male and one with a heavy Eastern European accent. Could it be Nikolai Mateev? He pressed into the metal, his cheek flat, his breath still, and heard no more.

Madelyn's grip on his hand tightened. In the darkness, her mouth was against his ear. Her hot breath washed over his neck. "Don't make me run," she whispered. "I need to fight as much as you do."

"Together," he said, "we'll take down these bastards."

"Together," she said.

He smiled. Gun drawn, Roman pushed the door open and stepped into the bar.

Oleg laughed at Nikolai's latest joke with more amusement than it deserved and winced at the sound of his own faked merriment. He lifted the half-full beer to his lips and emptied the glass in one swallow. The drink landed in his gut like a liquid bomb and Oleg smothered yet another belch with the side of his hand. He was becoming disgusting.

A warm glow radiated from his middle, ending at the tips of his slightly numb fingers. How many beers, he wondered, would it take before he no longer cared about the pain he would be forced to inflict on Madelyn? Two? Three? Twenty?

The more time passed, the more he loathed the upcoming encounter. He may have enjoyed hurting Madelyn before, but he wasn't twisted enough to enjoy killing her in cold blood.

Sometimes he had to block out parts of himself to do what needed to be done. But as he'd learned over time, violence was just part of business. To ingratiate himself with Nikolai, Oleg would do anything.

"Another?" Oleg lifted his glass.

"*Da, da.* Another." Nikolai still held his Denver Broncos duffel, clutching it to his chest. He handed over the empty glass, then set the bag on the floor. Until now, the bag had remained in Nikolai's grasp since arriving. To Oleg, it seemed odd. He wanted to ask about its contents. Drugs? Cash? Diamonds?

Moving to the end of the bar, he stopped. A form emerged from the shadows. The glasses slipped from Oleg's hands and shattered on the floor. Roman Black stepped into the light, his gun drawn. How was he still in Boulder? Madelyn told Oleg that he'd left town. She'd been so certain. He'd been so certain.

"Who is this?" Nikolai demanded.

Roman said, as he strode farther into the room, "I'm an operative with Rocky Mountain Justice and you, Nikolai Mateev, are in my custody."

"Rocky Mountain Justice," Nikolai echoed. "You let me be taken by RMJ? How could you, Oleg? *Predatel'skaya negodyay.*" *Traitorous wretch.* "You will die for this."

Oh hell. Oleg wished that Roman would shoot him now. It would save him from the agony that Nikolai Mateev promised to inflict. Where was the rest of the team from RMJ? Or the feds? Or even the cops? Surely, there had to be more of them.

But, no. No armed men rushed from the basement. The front door did not explode open, blown from its hinges by bits of charge.

Was it just Roman?

Oleg was trapped in a vise, squeezed by two deadly men. The need for self-preservation was like a thirst, but how long would he last—even in jail—if he made a deal with the law? No, he'd never betray his people, his calling, his destiny.

"Go, Otets," Oleg said. "Get out of here. Save yourself."

Roman twitched his barrel toward Nikolai. "Get on the floor, Mateev. Lie facedown and put your hands behind your head where I can see them."

Oleg glanced over his shoulder. The godfather of

the Russian Mafia looked not at Roman, the enemy, but at Oleg—his ally. He spat, hitting Oleg under the eye. Oleg flinched as if struck.

Nikolai kept his eyes on Oleg as he got slowly to his knees and then flattened on the ground. *"Predatel'skaya negodyay." Traitorous wretch.* He repeated.

"It wasn't me," Oleg said. "I swear. This man worked with Serge. He was part of the group meant to betray you."

"Shut up," Roman growled, "and save your excuses for the judge." Then over his shoulder, he called, "Madelyn."

Madelyn materialized from the shadows. Had Roman only returned for the woman, his timing impeccably bad? Was Oleg now the one who was in the wrong place at the wrong time?

"There's a phone behind the bar. I need you to make a call," Roman said.

She gave a wordless nod. Madelyn rested her hand on Roman's arm as she passed.

Madelyn. Oleg cursed her name. It was her death that was to be his salvation. And alive? She was his destruction. Or was she? He'd only get one chance to make this work. As she neared the bar, Madelyn glared at Oleg. For such a small person, she had a fierce persona. He smiled. She narrowed her eyes.

One more smile from Oleg. It was not returned, yet he didn't care. Oleg pivoted and grabbed Madelyn. Before she could scream or Roman could fire, he had one arm across her throat and the other at the back of her neck. "Put the gun down, Roman," he said.

Madelyn wheezed as she struggled for breath.

Roman advanced. "Let her go."

"You won't shoot me. To get to me you have to shoot through her." Oleg tightened his grip on Madelyn's throat, cutting off even more air. She reached for the constricting arm and pulled. She tried to turn her neck into the crease of his elbow. He held her head steady against the solid bone of his forearm. He tightened his grip, pressing harder into her larynx and her hands fell away. "If you don't drop the gun, I'll break her neck. Letting her die seems to be the one thing you refuse to do."

Roman didn't waver and Oleg began to sweat.

"Don't play with me," Oleg said. "I will break her neck. One. Two."

Pain erupted in Oleg's forearm and his hand went numb. He saw red. Red walls. Red floor. Red blood flowing out of a wound cut by a red knife. Madelyn dropped to her knees and stumbled toward Roman.

Oleg gripped his arm. A packing knife was in his flesh, driven in to the hilt by Madelyn's free hand. Blood seeped through his fingers. He dropped to his knees. In that instant, Nikolai rose, a black submachine gun in his hand. The barrel was short and the grip was tucked into his side. A long magazine, with more than one hundred bullets, hung down from the stock. Within a second, Nikolai could end every life in the room.

The Colorado Mustangs duffel lay open at Nikolai's feet. At least now Oleg knew what had been in the bag.

"You," Nikolai said to Oleg. "You and I will leave here and collect all my money."

"There's cash behind the bar. It's in a safe," said Oleg. "It's enough to get you out of town."

"I'm glad to see that my trust in you wasn't completely misplaced."

Despite the pain, Oleg couldn't help but smile. He should've known that it would all turn out in his favor. Greatness was in his blood and could not be ignored. He bit back a scream as he pried the knife from his arm and then tossed the blade aside. He stood and fished the car keys from his pocket, ready to start the next chapter of his life.

"Girl," Nikolai said to Madelyn. "Get my money."

"Bottom shelf," said Oleg. "Behind all the bottles, there's a trap door. It's in there."

Madelyn set all the bottles aside and had the trapdoor open within a minute. Oleg gave her the combination. With the safe open, Madelyn withdrew two stacks of bills—all C-notes—to the tune of one hundred thousand US dollars. She stood, the money in her hands.

To Oleg, it seemed as if each had something the other wanted. Madelyn held the money. Both Roman and Nikolai were armed—their guns trained on the other. Oleg had a means of escape.

"Come to me, girl," Nikolai said. "And bring my money."

The Russian still had his gun trained on Roman and Madelyn hesitated only a moment before coming from behind the bar and stepping in front of Nikolai. Hands full of bills, her arms were outstretched.

For Oleg, a million things happened separately and all at once. Madelyn tossed the stack of money in the air and bills surrounded them like a blizzard. She struck fast and precise. Reach. Twist. Break. Flip. The gun was in her hands, not Nikolai's. Mateev dropped to the floor and scrambled for the bills as they floated to the ground.

Upright again, Nikolai rushed for the door.

"Stop or I'll shoot," Roman said.

Nikolai didn't heed the warning.

Roman's finger moved to the trigger.

Oleg wasn't about to let his legacy be that of the man who led Rocky Mountain Justice to Nikolai Mateev. He was the descendant of the czars and knew when personal sacrifices needed to be made. He lunged forward, pushing Nikolai out of the line of fire. A stinging sensation drove through his back. Then another and another and another. He fell to the ground, his legs no longer under his command.

Nikolai bent to grasp the car keys from Oleg's open hand. Hurriedly, he pushed the front door open.

Oleg clawed to the filthy concrete outside. Above,

he saw an evening sky streaked with pink and red and purple. At the curb was his own car. Oleg watched as the most important man to come out of Russia since Stalin slid behind the driver's seat and sped away. Roman gave chase on foot. Two bullets were fired. *Pop. Pop.* Then the car rounded a corner and was gone. In the distance, he heard the wail of sirens.

The sun slid behind the buildings across the street. The last light of day blinded Oleg and he shut his eyes. He didn't feel the warmth of the rays, only the cold and biting wind of the Siberian plains. In the distance, he heard the howl of the wolves. And the howl of the wolves. And nothing.

Chapter 11

Oleg lay on a gurney, an oxygen mask covered his mouth. He was wheeled into the back of the ambulance and it sped away. The bodies of both Serge and Anton had been removed by the coroner only moments before. Even with those vehicles gone, the street in front of The Prow was still full of lights and people. A barricade had been set up at each end of the block. A mix of newscasters and neighbors huddled next to the barrier. They yelled questions to officials on the scene, trying to make sense of the situation.

Roman stood next to Madelyn. She was on another gurney at the rear of a second ambulance. A paramedic swabbed her face with an antiseptic wipe and she flinched.

"You okay?" Roman asked. It was an inane question to be sure, but all he had.

"I guess," she said. "What now?"

"You can go back home and never worry about Oleg Zavalov again."

"Not for me, but for you and the case?"

"Now every law enforcement officer in the country starts looking for Nikolai Mateev."

"I'm sorry that I went to see Ava. If I hadn't, then Nikolai wouldn't have gotten away."

"All of this has been awful for you, I know," Roman said. "But it is because of you that we have Oleg Zavalov in custody and know that Nikolai Mateev is somewhere close. It's only a matter of time before he's found."

"I feel I made the wrong choice twice over, and ruined everything."

Her words of contrition squeezed Roman's heart. "You don't know what would have happened or not. None of us owns a crystal ball," he said. "And if we did, then we'd play the lottery and retire to an island."

She laughed a little. It was exactly what he needed to hear.

Still in a suit and tie, Ian Wallace approached at a fast clip. He cut through the knot of uniformed police officers and crime scene technicians in their nylon blue windbreakers.

"It's been a hell of a day for you two."

"What's going on in there?"

"Oleg Zavalov's computer has been opened. It

seems he hacked into the cellular network and had record of Ms. Thompkins's final cell tower contact near the turnoff by the bridge. I assume it's how he found the safe house."

"How'd he get my number?" Madelyn asked.

If Roman was a betting man, he'd wager that Oleg had gotten it from Ava. But he didn't need to add to Madelyn's heartache over her sister. "He's good with computers," Roman said. "There's very little he couldn't have found."

Madelyn shrugged. "I guess." Maybe she suspected Ava, as well.

"Anything else?" Roman asked.

"There is," said Ian. He held up an evidence bag with three prescription bottles inside. "We found these in the duffel bag belonging to Nikolai Mateev. Of course, they'll be analyzed at the lab, but since you're a doctor, I was hoping you could tell me what they might be used to treat?"

Ian handed the bag to Madelyn and she looked through the translucent plastic. "This one is for nausea. And these two are immune boosters." With a sigh, she handed the bag back. "It's a pretty typical regimen for cancer patients undergoing chemo."

"Cancer?" asked Ian. "Nikolai Mateev has cancer?"

"It makes sense if you think about it," Roman said. "His sudden need for an heir—first his grandson and then his great-nephew. More than that, the United States has advanced medical care, so he might come here for treatment. Finding any newly filled prescriptions for these drugs could help locate Nikolai."

"An interesting thought," said Ian, "and one that I promise to act on. Since Oleg's car was found abandoned seven blocks west of here, we need to be creative in our search efforts. You're a hell of an intel officer, Roman. I hope you plan to stay on this case to the end."

Roman accepted with a nod, although there was no way they were going to take this case from him. "And Oleg? How is he?"

"He's on his way to the hospital now, but things don't look good."

Roman had seen enough battlefield trauma to know that a human body could withstand serious injuries and survive. Yet, he'd also seen enough to know that Oleg was close to that limit. "To me, it looked like he sacrificed himself so that Mateev could get away."

"Maybe there is honor among criminals. Or maybe it was easier to get shot by the cops than to have Nikolai order jailhouse justice. Who knows, at least Oleg's not part of the equation anymore."

"At all?" asked Madelyn.

"Oleg's influence in the criminal underworld was based on his family's association with Nikolai Mateev. And if he loses Nikolai's blessing, which he might after all this...? Let's just say that he won't be able to rouse too many thugs to his aid," Roman said. "On the off chance that he survives, he'll be in prison for the rest of his life and you'll be safe."

Madelyn exhaled and nodded. "That's a relief. And what about Ava?"

"She's being held at the University of Colorado Hospital in a detox unit," said Ian. "But your sister is technically in custody of the Boulder City Police Department as an accessory to your kidnapping."

"My sister's not a criminal," said Madelyn. "She needs help. Is there any way I can speak to her?"

"I'll see what I can do," Ian said. He withdrew his phone and typed out a text. "Hopefully, the hospital will approve."

"And what about Jackson?" Roman asked. "He's the Boulder PD officer who frequented The Prow."

"He's cooperating fully with authorities, but I don't know what will become of him," Ian said. The phone in his hand beeped. He looked at the screen. "Good news, Madelyn. You're able to speak to your sister."

"When?"

"As soon as you can be transported," Ian said.

As if on cue, two paramedics stepped forward. "Excuse me, sir. We need to get this patient to the hospital. Doctor's orders." One lifted Madelyn's gurney into the back of the ambulance and followed. The other shut the door and rounded to the front, getting into the driver's seat.

The ambulance maneuvered through the police

barricade. Once on the street, it gathered speed before disappearing around the corner.

Roman stood in the middle of the road, staring. People walked by, jostling him as they passed. He'd never been more alone in his life.

Ian clapped a hand on his shoulder. "You okay?"

Roman shook his head.

"Let's get you checked out, too. Come on, I'll give you a ride to the hospital."

"I'm fine," he said. His words a faint echo of his feelings. "It's just…"

"It's just, what?"

Roman looked away from the place where the ambulance had turned. "It's just that I think I let the best thing that ever happened to me walk out of my life."

Upon arriving at the hospital, Madelyn had been ordered to remain in a wheelchair until she'd been thoroughly evaluated. But first, she was given the opportunity to see Ava. A visit such as this was uncommon. Madelyn supposed it was a perk of being enrolled in the hospital's teaching program. An orderly pushed Madelyn down that hall, stopping in front of a door that was unremarkable except for the police officer stationed outside.

"You have five minutes," the officer said to Madelyn. "And if you need me, just call. I'll be right here the whole time."

"Thanks," she said, as the orderly wheeled her into the room, retreated and shut the door behind him.

Ava lay on the bed, staring at the ceiling. A white sheet and blanket were folded across her chest. An IV was attached to one arm. Several bags of clear fluids hung from a pole and dripped medications into the tubing. Ava's other arm was handcuffed to the bed.

Madelyn sat in silence, not sure how she felt or what she wanted to say.

"I guess you came to yell at me." Ava cast her gaze to Madelyn and then back at the ceiling.

"No," said Madelyn.

"You aren't mad at me?"

Madelyn gave a snort. "I'm so far beyond mad that you can't see mad in the rearview mirror."

"So, you did come to yell."

"Would it do any good?"

"Probably not," said Ava. She paused a beat. "Why did you come?"

"To make sure that you're okay." She paused. "I talked to Mom and Dad for a second and let them know you're in the hospital. They want to know how you're doing."

Ava rattled her handcuffed wrist. "I'm splendid. Thank your boyfriend for having me arrested. It'll be fun to talk about when the family gets together next Thanksgiving."

Madelyn hadn't expected contrition, or even an apology. Yet, she didn't have the stomach for Ava playing the defiant victim.

"Ava, you're my sister and I will always love you, no matter what you do. I want to help you. If you ever care to accept that help, let me know." Madelyn pushed the wheels on her chair back, maneuvering toward the door.

"I don't want my life to be like this, you know."

Madelyn stopped. "I know."

"I am sorry, Maddie. I don't know why I did what I did. I didn't really know what kind of person Oleg Zavalov was, you know?" Ava took in a shaking breath. "That's not true, I do know. I wanted drugs—the next high is all I think about. It frees me from my own body, my own life, and all the crappy things I've done. Getting high is all I care about sometimes. But I do love you, too."

Turning back to her sister, Madelyn wheeled next to the bed and reached for Ava's hand.

"Can you forgive me?" Ava asked.

Could she? Ava's quest for easy drugs had almost cost Madelyn her life several times over. More than that, there was the constant worry and the heartache to their parents. Ava should be told and held accountable for it all. Madelyn recoiled, shocked by her own thoughts. Had she come to gloat? She refused to be that kind of person.

Madelyn squeezed Ava's hand tighter. "I forgive you, Ava."

Tears streamed down Ava's cheeks. She lifted her hand to wipe them away. The handcuff rattled and Ava's arm jerked to a stop. Madelyn grabbed a tissue and dabbed her sister's eyes.

The door opened and the orderly entered. "Time's up," he said.

Madelyn lifted from the seat and kissed her sister on the forehead. "I love you, Ava."

Still crying, Ava smiled. "Maybe this time it'll be okay."

Madelyn sank back into the wheelchair and gave a little wave. Maybe this time Ava was right and it would work out just fine.

Madelyn reclined on the hospital bed, feeling healthy and ready to be released. All she needed was to be given the results before being allowed to go home. The story of the shoot-out at The Prow had hit the press, so she called her parents a second time and gave them a complete rundown of the events before they heard about it on the news. They were on their way from Cheyenne. Both were horrified for what she'd endured, but thankful that Ava was once again undergoing treatment.

It seemed that every person with whom Madelyn had worked—even briefly—had stopped by for a visit. Far from finding the constant parade of companionship annoying, Madelyn felt cared for and respected. There was one person who she wanted to see and he had yet to arrive: Roman. At this late hour, she doubted that he would come.

Madelyn turned to the window, the world outside dark. She wondered how much longer she'd be asked to wait—never mind how she'd get home if the buses were no longer running.

"Knock, knock." A familiar voice came from the doorway. Roman leaned a shoulder on the doorjamb, one foot crossed over the other. A white hospital band encircled one wrist and he held the canvas bag she'd gotten at RMJ filled with her clothes. "I wanted to return this to you," he said as he entered her room. "I figured it'd be best to give them to you now, since we're both here."

"Sure," she said, swallowing down a huge helping of disappointment that he'd only come to return her shirt and jacket. "Thanks."

"Do you have a minute?"

Here it comes—The Speech. She knew the one. It was where Roman told her how she was an amazing person, but that she was too focused and ambitious, and there was no room in her life for anyone else. Did guys not understand how badly it hurt to be rejected for having goals? It was why she'd given him all those excuses already.

Roman sat on the edge of her bed. "You're an amazing person," he said. "I've met anyone with the same amount of drive or determination as you."

She wanted to laugh or cry or maybe throw up. No matter how badly Madelyn wanted a career in medicine, or how much more she'd need to sacrifice to get it—she could not hear Roman give her The Speech.

She held up her hand, halting his words. "But," she continued for him. "But. But. But my life plan is so set that it's hard for you to see a place where you'd fit. I was right all along. You don't need to explain yourself. Really."

"I'm not letting you push me away," he said. "I have goals, too. But when I didn't know where you were or what Oleg had done to you. Well, it was the worst moment of my life."

It took a second for his words to make sense and even then, Madelyn could hardly believe what he'd said. "I'm not sure I understand."

"The only way I won't fit into your life is if you don't want to make a place for me. I'm not going to give up on us, so get used to seeing me around. That's what I came to tell you."

Roman reached for her hands, clasping both of hers between his own. "Madelyn, I love how you're competent and don't back down from any challenge. I love how you work twice as hard as anyone else and don't need to be praised for your accomplishments. I love how you'll risk everything for someone you care about—although from now on—you can ask me for help."

Tears filled her eyes and her chest tightened with emotion. "You do?"

"I want to be with you," Roman said. "I don't want to take care of you, I want us to take care of each other. Madelyn, what I'm trying to say is that I'm in love with you."

"After a day?"

"Well, it has been a weird day…"

* * *

Roman held himself completely still. It had been a little more than two weeks since the shoot-out at The Prow and that part of the Mateev case had been closed. Yet, Roman found himself at another pivotal moment.

Madelyn was at his side and he reached for her hand.

"How long has it been?" he asked.

"About thirty seconds since you asked last time," she said. There was a smile in her voice.

"Long enough, right?"

He grabbed the white, plastic tube from the bathroom counter. He peered at the opaque screen. It had one word on it: pregnant.

"A baby," he said, drawing Madelyn into his embrace. His chest tightened with emotion. A moment like this had, not so long ago, seemed alien. Now it was the most natural feeling in the world. "You're the best thing that's ever happened to me. I want us to be together always."

"Are you sure that's what you want?" she asked, pulling away slightly and looking at up at him. "To raise a baby with me? Medical school is hard enough, and babies definitely don't sleep much either. Are you sure you know what you're signing up for, Soldier?"

He kissed the top of her head, loving her sense of humor. "There's nothing I want more. I was born for this mission."

Epilogue

Oleg's mouth was dry. His throat was raw. His chest burned. He wondered if these physical tortures meant that he had finally died and gone to hell. A rhythmic *beep, beep, beep* matched the sluggish beating of his heart and Oleg knew that Death had rejected him a second time, throwing him back to the living.

He would've preferred hell.

"Mr. Zavalov? Can you hear me?" a man with a British accent asked. Maybe he was dead. Oleg always imagined that the Devil would be English. Satan continued, "My name is Sir Ian Wallace."

Oleg opened one eye. A blond man wearing a navy suit and yellow tie stood at his bedside. He'd have preferred to find the Devil. Oleg tried to tell the proper Brit to properly sod off. His words came out gurgled.

"You have a breathing tube down your throat," Sir Ian said. "Until that's removed, you won't be able to speak." Ian placed a pen in Oleg's hand and set a legal pad on his stomach. "There are a great many charges that will be filed against you. Colorado is a de facto capital punishment state and nobody has been executed in years. Exceptions will be made in your case. Then there are a bevy of federal charges that also hold the death penalty. If you care to live, albeit in prison, you need to share what you know about Nikolai Mateev."

Oleg scribbled two words on the page.

"Get away?" Ian read. "Do you mean Nikolai? Are you asking if Mr. Mateev got away?"

Oleg nodded.

"Yes, he did. Do you know where he might have gone?"

If Oleg gave information to RMJ about Nikolai Mateev, he was as good as dead. Oleg wrote one word. "No."

"Are you sure? Right now, the media believes you to be deceased. You can stay that way and go to prison under an alias. If not, well, let's just say that Nikolai Mateev has enough influence, especially in the penal system, to take care of any problem in any jail in this country. I assume he'd consider you to be a problem, but not if he knew nothing about you."

He wrote another word.

"Parole?" said Sir Ian. "Are you asking if you could be paroled?"

Oleg nodded.

"I'm afraid not. The only thing you can get is anonymity in jail and no death penalty."

Oleg set the pen on the pad of paper and pushed both aside. He let his eyes close and began to pray for death.

Ian stepped into the hallway of the University of Colorado's hospital. FBI special agent Marcus Jones waited for him. "And?" he asked as Ian closed the door to Oleg Zavalov's room.

Ian shook his head. "He has nothing to say."

"You gave him the offer? A new identity and life in prison versus the death penalty."

"I did," said Ian. "He wasn't interested."

He handed Marcus the legal pad. Only a single page held a few words of Oleg's shaky scrawl. Special Agent Jones glanced at the legal pad before handing it back.

He leaned against the wall and rubbed his eyes with the heel of his hands. "Oleg is loyal, I'll give him that."

"Or possibly delusional, but it doesn't matter any longer," said Ian. "Nikolai Mateev. He's our real target."

"What do we do now?" Jones stepped away from the wall and walked down the corridor.

Ian fell in step with Marcus. "One of our operatives had a unique thought. We all agree that Nikolai Mateev has cancer, yes?"

"Well, we haven't gotten the results from the lab. The pills in the bottle might not match the prescriptions."

"But assuming they do…"

"Assuming they do," Marcus repeated. "Sure."

"We can start by looking for newly filled prescriptions."

"It's a unique place to start," said Jones. "I can't believe that Nikolai Mateev slipped through our fingers. It makes me sick."

"We underestimated him," Ian said. "And what's worse is he knew we would. But don't worry. There's no place that Nikolai Mateev can hide where the men and women at Rocky Mountain Justice aren't willing to search. We'll find him."

"Is that a promise?" Special Agent Jones asked.

Ian shook his head. "More like a guarantee."

* * * * *

LET'S TALK
Romance

For exclusive extracts, competitions
and special offers, find us online:

 facebook.com/millsandboon

 @millsandboonuk

 @millsandboon

Or get in touch on 0844 844 1351*

For all the latest titles coming soon, visit
millsandboon.co.uk/nextmonth

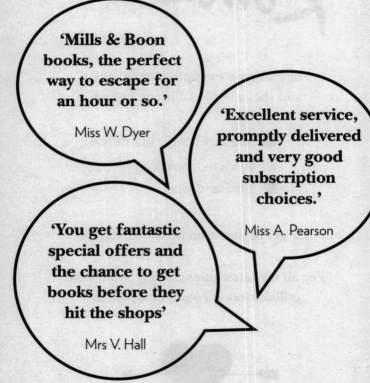